Her
HUSBAND, MY
SAVAGE
3

A NOVEL BY

CHARMANIE SAQUEA

Royalty Publishing House is now accepting manuscripts from aspiring or experienced urban romance authors!

WHAT MAY PLACE YOU ABOVE THE REST:

Heroes who are the ultimate book bae: strong-willed, maybe a little rough around the edges but willing to risk it all for the woman he loves.

Heroines who are the ultimate match: the girl next door type, not perfect - has her faults but is still a decent person. One who is willing to risk it all for the man she loves.

The rest is up to you! Just be creative, think out of the box, keep it sexy and intriguing!

If you'd like to join the Royal family, send us the first 15K words (60 pages) of your completed manuscript to submissions@royaltypublishinghouse.com

ACKNOWLEDGMENTS

First, I would like to thank God for blessing me with the talent of being an author. Here I am on book number 38; none of this would have been possible without Him.

To my mommy, Sheree, who has been by my side since day one. You told me I could be anything I wanted to be if I put my mind to it. You have always been my backbone, and I would not have made it this far without you. Also, my Grammy, you've been there every step of the way, and I can't thank you two enough.

My SONshine, Mykail, who will forever be greatest inspiration.

A HUGEEE thank you and shout out to Porscha and everyone at Royalty. You all are awesome! The love and support is miraculous.

I definitely can't forget to thank all the loyal readers who have been riding with me since *Official Girl*. You guys have been my motivation to keep going and busting my pen. All the inboxes, comments, and wall posts have never gone unnoticed, and I appreciate them and you more than you will ever know.

Last but never least, my angels in heaven, Cora (Mom), Romney (Riggz) and Marisa, Uncle Tyrone (Big Shep), and Dad. I pray that you continue to watch over me. I can't forget my cousin Tyrein; keep your head up baby… your time will be here before you know it.

Carmilla

*S*urprise, bitch. I know you're probably flipping out right now, wondering how and why. You really shouldn't be too surprised though. Did y'all really think I was going to let this man live happily ever after? With another bitch? Not by a long shot. Dillinger toyed with my heart before ripping it out of my chest and playing basketball with it and slam dunking it right in the damn trash.

He must've forgot that my daddy was a judge and I had connections as well as knew how to pull some strings to make shit happen. I kept my eyes trained on Dillinger as he sat there stagnant, not showing any emotion, but that was fine because I knew he was going crazy on the inside. He wasn't expecting this, and that was what I took pride in the most.

He thought he could play me for a fool, not knowing the joke was going to be on him in the end. He underestimated me and my abilities, and *that* was his biggest downfall.

"And how do you know the defendant, Mrs. Rivera?"

"He's my husband," I spoke.

Yes, Dillinger and I were in fact still married. I refused to sign the divorce papers. There was no way in hell I was going to let him just walk away from me like that. Since he didn't want to spend the rest of his life with me, enjoying his freedom, he could spend the rest of his life as a ward of the fucking state.

A crooked smile formed on my face as I thought about what I did to land myself in this stand, testifying on my own husband.

It had been a little over an hour since Dillinger had presented me with the divorce papers and had all my belongings dropped off to my parents' house. To say that I was hurt would undeniably be an under-statement. Not only was I hurt, but I was embarrassed, more so humili-ated. He had delivered two severe low blows by asking for the divorce and basically kicking me out of his house.

"Carmilla, what—"

"Not right now." I cut my mom off from saying whatever she was about to let fly out of her mouth.

"I was just—"

"Mom, I said not right now!" I bellowed out.

I was already emotional, considering the events that had just taken place, and I knew she didn't want to do anything but further antagonize me. This was exactly what I didn't need. Something else to prove to her that her least favorite child couldn't do shit right. She was definitely going to have a field day with telling my sister Carmen about this one.

Basically, my whole life, I had been trying to do everything I could to shut my sister and my mom up. Nothing I did would live up to her precious Carmen. That bitch could do no wrong in our mother's eyes. Literally, everything I did was compared to my older sister.

I couldn't tell you how many times I had to hear dumb shit like

"Well, Carmen graduated from law school." Or "Well, Carmen got married right out of college." I was so sick of this shit.

"What's going on in here?" my dad asked, perplexed about my outburst.

"I was trying to console your daughter, and she just wants to take all her anger and frustrations out on me."

I rolled my eyes at the bullshit spewing out of her mouth. She knew damn well she was not trying to console me. Taunt me, maybe, but certainly not console. Never, since I'd been on this earth, could I ever remember a time when my own mother had ever comforted me.

"Just leave her alone, Sharon. I'm pretty sure she doesn't want to be bothered right now; she's already going through enough." My daddy defended me, seeing right through his wife's bullshit.

"Daddy, I need someone's number," I told him as I followed him back to his office.

"Who might that be, sweetheart?" he asked.

"Your friend, Detective Marshall. I have some information for him," I told my daddy.

I was done playing with Dillinger. I had let him get away with too much, but I was not going to allow him to get away with this shit. He was sadly mistaken if he thought I was going to let him just run off into the sunset with his little side whore.

My dad sat back in his chair and looked at me with uncertainty. I already knew what he was thinking, but there was nothing he could say to me that would deter me. I had already made up in my mind what I was going to do.

"Honey, are you sure this is what you want to do? You're not thinking clearly right now, and you're acting off of emotions. Why don't you just go lay down? It's been a very eventful day for you. I'm sure you could use the rest," my daddy told me.

"The number please?" I said, ignoring everything he'd just said.

Sighing heavily, he reached in the drawer of his desk and came up with a book. After flipping through a few pages, he wrote something down and handed it to me. I took the paper from him, quickly scanning over the number he had written down.

Before he could open his mouth to say another word, I did an about face, walking out of his office and to my room. Picking up my phone, I quickly dialed the number my daddy gave me before I placed the phone to my ear, anxiously waiting for him to answer.

"Hello—"

"Detective Marshall, this is Carmilla Pennington... Rivera, and I have some information regarding Chad Drummer's death," I informed him.

"Really? Would you like to come down to the station so we could discuss what information you have?" he asked.

"Sure. I'll be there in about twenty minutes," I let him know.

After ending our phone conversation, I sighed. I hated to have to do this, but Dillinger had pushed me to this point. Had he just loved me and been faithful in our marriage, like he was supposed to, we wouldn't have to be going through this.

Snapping out of my thoughts, I focused my attention back on what was happening now. Paul, the prosecutor, was a friend of my fathers as well. As I stated before, I knew people in high places, and there was no way in hell that Dillinger was getting out of this one.

After Paul finished with his line of questioning, he sat back in his seat while I sat on the witness stand with a satisfied smirk. Dillinger's lawyer stood up, and I had to admit that she was beautiful. She stood about five feet nine with a flawless mocha skin complexion that was blemish free. The pantsuit she wore hugged her body, but I doubted she would be able to hide her figure regardless of what she was, because she was stacked. Her thick hair was bone straight, parted down the middle and hanging down her shoulders.

She gave me a smile that didn't reach her eyes.

"Ms. Rivera... excuse me, *Mrs.* Rivera, how long have you been with Mr. Rivera?" she asked.

"We've been together for five years, but we've been married for roughly nine and a half months," I answered.

"Hmm, so you were being intimate with Mr. Rivera while you were still in a relationship with Mr. Drummer, correct?"

4

"Objection, your honor! " Paul exclaimed as he jumped up out of his seat. "Relevance?"

I cut my eyes in Dillinger's direction, and he was sitting there with a crooked smirk on his face. If I could go down there and slap it off his face, I swear I would.

"I'll allow it," Judge Cramebrooke said. "Answer the question, Mrs. Rivera."

"No. Dillinger and I were not intimate until after I officially broke things off with Chad." I corrected her.

She just nodded her head. "Five years is quite a long run to be with someone. You know your husband very well, huh? Better than anyone, would you say?"

"Yes. I know Dillinger very well. Better than anyone." I answered with confidence.

"So why did you find it a shock when Mr. Drummer revealed to you about my client's troubled past? Records that were supposed to be sealed, might I add."

"Because that was just one snippet of his life that Dillinger had failed to mention to me," I let her know.

"Hmm, the man who you've been with for five years and know better than anyone, failed to tell you about his past? Very well then." She shrugged.

I knew exactly what she was trying to do. She was trying to make it seem as if I didn't know Dillinger like that. Granted, that may have been so, but I wasn't going to allow her to play me and try to have me up here looking like a damn fool.

"Mrs. Rivera, why did you wait so long to tell your husband about the threats Mr. Drummer threatened you with?" she asked as she slightly cocked her head to the side.

"Because I was afraid," I said truthfully.

"Afraid of what?"

"Afraid of what Dillinger might do," I answered.

"Were you afraid of what he might do when you willingly texted him the information on how and where to find the deceased?" she asked.

"Objection, your honor! She's badgering the witness!" Paul exclaimed.

"Withdrawn. No further questions, your honor," she said as she sat down.

Before she could even sit down good, Dillinger was leaning over, whispering something in her ear. Whatever he said caused a big smile to spread across her face. I couldn't hide the look of disgust even if I wanted to. It was clear that they were going to try to spin this, but that was okay; I loved playing dirty.

Layla

"*B*itch, what!" I exclaimed into the phone through a whisper. Cherokee had just finished telling me the events that had taken place at Dillinger's trial. Even though it was my day off, I had gotten called into work due to one of my boys having a crisis. Therefore, I couldn't go to court today, but my bestie wasted no time filling me in on what happened.

To say that my mouth was on the floor would be putting it lightly. I couldn't believe Carmilla had pulled a grimy ass move like that on Dillinger. I knew hell hath no fury like a woman scorned, but that bitch was straight ruthless for the stunt she pulled.

"Yes, Lay. She walked in there with pride at the shit she was doing," Cherokee spat in disdain.

"I'm happy I didn't come then. I would've been found in contempt and locked up for beating her ass right there in the courtroom. Dillinger and I may not be on the best of terms right now, but she too disrespectful," I told Cherokee.

Ever since that scene he caused at the hospital when Santos got shot, Dillinger's and my relationship had been shaky. I always looked at him like a big brother, even when he was in a relationship with Carmilla. Not once did I disrespect her or their relationship. He obviously felt some type of way and couldn't show me the same respect.

I pulled the phone away from my ear when I got a text notification.

Jacier: *I left yo key under the mat at yo crib. It's been real and ain't no love lost on my end. Maybe next lifetime, A'Layla.*

I swallowed the lump that had formed in my throat as my hands suddenly became clammy. I read the message about five times in disbelief. I was certain that I had read it wrong, so I had to keep reading it. When I realized that Jacier was saying exactly what I was afraid of, it caused my heart to break.

"Hellooooo, Lay!" Cherokee said into the phone.

"He... he's gone," I said just above a whisper.

"What? Who's gone?" she asked in a panic.

I realized she must've thought I was talking about Santos, so I quickly clarified who and what I was talking about.

"Jacier... He left me."

Granted, it had been a little over a week since we had a little blowup and he found out I was going up there to visit Santos every day. I knew he was pissed when he refused to stay at my house like he had been doing since we'd been together and opted to stay at his own home instead.

I knew he was pissed with me, but I really felt like he was being extra as hell right now.

"Left you? What are you talking about, Layla? Stop playing. That man did not leave you," she said.

It suddenly hit me that I didn't tell her about Jacier finding out about what I was doing, because I didn't want to hear I told you so. I screenshot the text he just sent me, sending it to Cherokee before telling her to check her phone. She was quiet for a few before I heard her let out a gasp.

"Lay, what—"

"He found out about me going to see Santos. How he found out, I don't know, but he did. He basically told me that he felt like I didn't really want to be with him because my heart was still with Santos. He left that day, and I haven't seen him since. Mind you, this was over a week ago. My phone calls and texts have all been ignored. Then he sends me this text out the blue." I explained the short version to her.

The line got quite so I had to pull the phone away from my face to make sure she hadn't hung up since I didn't hear the three beeps indicating that the call had ended. When I saw the timer telling me how long we had been on the phone, I contorted my face in confusion while placing the phone back to my ear.

"Uhh, hello?"

"A'Layla, I'm never the one to kick somebody when they're down, but as your best friend, I'm obligated to always keep it real with you, no matter what. I told you to tell Jacier about you going to see Santos from the jump. I even told you to tell him when you came by the workplace. Did I not?"

"Yes," I answered, feeling like a child being scolded by its mother.

"Okay then. You had to know that Jacier was going to feel some type of way about the situation. Just think, Lay. The same thing you left Santos for is exactly what you are doing in your relationship with Jacier. Granted, you're not hiding a child from him, but the fact still remains you were hiding *something* from him. You told me you didn't want any secrets, remember? I love you, Lay, but I can't condone this one. Jacier is a good man, and it would be a shame if you missed out on him because you don't know how to leave the past in the past," Cherokee said, sounding like Iyanla Vanzant or somebody.

"You're right. Let me call you back though," I said as I hung up before she could say anything else.

Once I ended the phone call with her, I hit Jacier's name in my recent calls to FaceTime him. I had to pick my face up off the floor when he didn't answer. Jacier *always* answered the phone for me, no matter if he was in the middle of something or not. He always liked to tell me that no matter how busy a person was, if they really wanted you, they would make time for you. Putting my pride to the side, I called him again, but this time, it was a regular phone call. I placed the phone to my ear. It rang three times on my end before I heard his sexy voice.

"Waddup?"

"Wow, but you couldn't answer my FaceTime?" I questioned, feeling slighted.

"Naw, I couldn't," he stated. "I'm driving."

"Where are you going?"

"Does it really matter?" Jacier asked.

I had to blink multiple times to keep the tears that wanted to fall at bay. Jacier was being so cold toward me right now that the shit was actually giving me chills. He had never been anything but gentle with me, even before we decided to make it official. Jacier had never acted like that with me.

I could hear him sighing deeply before he chose to speak again. "I'm going to Atlanta," he told me in a much softer tone. "I think I'm gon' be gone for a while. I got some loose end to tie up. Like I told you in the text though, ain't no love lost on my end."

"So that's it? You're not going to hear me out? We can't talk about this?" I asked, perplexed.

"What is there to talk about, A'Layla? I'm tired of talking to you, because the shit is getting me nowhere with you. You had all the opportunity in the world to talk and to tell me you was sneaking up there to see that nigga, but you didn't, so why we gotta talk now?" he inquired.

"I didn't know how to tell you, Jacier. I—"

"You didn't know how to tell me because you know like I know that the nigga ain't all the way out yo' system. No matter how much I try to show you how much of a real nigga I am, the shit will be to no avail because I'm not where you wanna be. You can try to deny it all you want to, but your actions prove otherwise. I gotta go though."

Before I could even get a word in, Jacier had ended the call. The tears I had fought hard to keep at bay had fallen. I covered my mouth with my hand as I tried to keep myself from breaking down. Did I really just lose what possibly could've been the best thing to ever happen to me?

My phone started ringing, and I rushed to answer it, thinking it was Jacier calling me back, but instead, it was the hospital. Wiping my face, I pulled myself together to answer the phone.

"Hello, Ms. Mathis. This is Doctor Pine, Rahiem's doctor. How are you today?" he said into the phone.

I swallowed the lump that had formed in my throat, hoping he wasn't calling me with some bad news. I had left my number with him, with instructions to call me if there were any changes in his condition.

"How I'm doing all depends on what you're calling me about, Dr. Pine," I let him know.

"Well, you told me to give you a call if there were any changes. I just wanted to inform you that Rahiem is woke and alert," he said, surprising the hell out of me.

I said a silent prayer, thanking God for keeping Santos and bringing him back to us.

3

Santos

$\mathcal{I}$ gave the cute ass nurse a smile as she brought the water I had asked for. The tight ass scrubs she had on, showed off her perfect figure. She had just the right amount of hips, thighs, and ass. Even her titties were big, and I could imagine burying my face in between them. She moved about the room, checking all the machines I was hooked up to, paying me no damn attention at all. When she turned her body, I got a better look at her round homegrown ass. I could tell it was all natural because she had the perfect hip and thigh proportion. I was stuck in a trance until I heard the sound of little pitter patter and Reign running in my direction.

"Daddy!" she yelled excitedly.

The nurse gave her a big smile as I swooped her up in my arms, placing kisses all over her face. I expected to see Cherokee coming in behind her, but I damn near fell out the hospital bed when I saw Layla instead.

"Yeah, I'm here now," she said into the phone as she walked in the room. "Okay... here," she said as she handed me her phone.

I took it with a raised brow before placing it to my ear. "Hello?" I answered.

"Welcome back, brother!" Cherokee's voice boomed through the phone.

I had to laugh at her loud ass. "Thanks, sis. Where the hell you at?" I asked as I picked up my cup of water.

The ice-cold water was so soothing as it went down my throat. I kept my eyes trained on Layla as she walked to the other side of the room, standing in front of the window.

"I had to take care of some business with one of my clients, but I promise to be there as soon as I'm done," Cherokee told me.

"You better," I told her as we ended the phone call.

"Daddy, I missed you," Reign said as she rubbed her small hand over my cheek.

"I missed you too, baby. I hope you been being a good girl."

"I have! Ain't I been a good girl, Lay Lay?" she asked with a bright smile as she turned to look at Layla.

Pulling her attention from the window, she turned to look at Reign, matching her smile.

"Of course you have, baby," Layla told her as she walked over to retrieve her phone.

"You like my nails, Daddy?" Reign asked as she held her hands up for me to see the pretty blue nail polish she had on.

"Yes, baby girl. They're very pretty, just like you," I told her.

"Lay Lay picked the color. I wanted mine just like hers." Reign beamed brightly.

I glanced at Layla's nails, and sure enough, she was sporting the same blue nail polish on her claws. I shot her a questioning look, and she just shrugged her shoulders while moving back to the other side of the room.

"Well, Lay Lay has some good taste, huh?" I asked as I started tickling her.

Reign let out a roaring laughter that I had missed so much. I couldn't wait to get out of this damn hospital so I could hit the streets and get at the nigga that called himself trying to take me from my daughter. I hoped Layla had all the fun she could with her little fuck boy because that nigga was a dead one. I may not have seen the nigga that filled my body with lead, but I had no doubts that he was the one responsible.

Besides Maino, I didn't have any beef with niggas out here. Unless he was sending hits from hell, I knew it wasn't him. That nigga wasn't slick though. I knew it was an act of revenge for me trying to kill his ass. I was still appalled at the fact that this nigga was still walking and breathing. I had never got at a nigga and he lived to tell it. That shit real life had me flabbergasted.

"Why you sitting all the way over there?" I asked Layla.

She had her face planted in her phone, not paying me any mind.

"I'm just here so Reign can see you. That's it, that's all. When Cherokee gets here, I'll be going on about my business," she said, not once looking up from her phone.

"You—"

"Talk to your daughter, Rahiem. I don't have nothing to say to you," she spat, still not bothering to look up from that raggedy ass phone.

I wanted to say something to her little ass, but the fact that Reign was sitting right here, I went ahead and swallowed all the obscenities I was ready to spew at her. Whether she wanted to or not, she was going to have to talk to me sooner rather than later.

* * *

"Damn, that bitch testified against him?" I asked, completely shocked.

Cherokee had just finished filling me in on everything I had been missing out on while being in a coma. I knew something had to be up when Dillinger didn't make his way up here to see me. We may not had been on the best of terms before the shooting, only speaking if business was involved, but we wasn't no petty ass niggas. When one of us was in need, we knew how to put our differences and bullshit to the side.

I still couldn't believe that they had locked Dillinger up for that bullshit. How the fuck you go from saying the shit was a suicide to looking him up for murder.

"Yes. He could possibly be spending the rest of his life behind bars because of a bitter bitch," Cherokee spat with fury.

"Then why the hell they ain't lock her dumb ass up for being an accessory? After all, she did give Dilly the info on how to get at that nigga."

Cherokee sucked her teeth and rolled her eyes before placing a handful of Doritos in her mouth. Her greedy and pregnant ass had her feet kicked up on the couch that was in my hospital room, with snacks surrounding her.

"She tried to play the role like she was scared of him. Talking about she feared what he might've done to her if she didn't give him the info," Cherokee said dryly.

"That bitch gotta be stopped." I shook my head.

"Yeah, she does."

Something about the way she said that caused me to look at her with a frown. I could literally see the wheels spinning around in her head.

"The hell you over there thinking about?" I asked.

"Let's just say I got murder on my mind," Cherokee said as she started rapping the lyrics to YNW Melly's hit song "Murder On My Mind."

I doubled over in laughter at her goofy ass. I made sure not to laugh too loud so I didn't wake up Reign, who was sleeping next to me in the hospital bed.

"Girl, shut the hell up. You ain't no damn killer," I reminded her.

"Neither was Tupac until you pushed him," she said with all seriousness.

15

I stopped and looked at her real good. Gone was the laughter and playfulness I had before, when I realized that she was serious as hell.

"Aye, chill the fuck out, Cherokee," I told her. "That nigga will kill you if you go out there and do something foolish and let something happen to you or his jit," I let her know.

"He don't have to know." She shrugged.

"Stop playing with me."

"Who said I'm playing?" she asked.

I just shook my head because I don't know what the hell had gotten into her.

"Cherokee, leave that shit alone. Let me handle it," I said. She just looked at me, but she didn't bother to respond. "Do you hear me talking to you?" I asked.

"Yeah." She mumbled before shoving some more chips into her mouth.

She may have thought this shit was a game, but it wasn't. No matter how many gangster flicks or how many of them damn books she read, the fact of the matter was Cherokee wasn't a damn killer. There was no way in hell I was going to allow her to be tainted like that. I knew she wanted to help Dillinger, but that wasn't the way to do it.

4

Cherokee

"*B*itch, are you crazy!" Layla yelled louder than I needed her to.

I had just finished telling her my plans for tonight, and now she was acting a damn fool. I slowly sipped my strawberry lemonade as my eyes scanned the restaurant we were currently sitting in. I chose to tell her here because I was sure she wouldn't act out in public, but who the hell was I kidding. This was A'Layla fucking Mathis I was talking about.

"Will you shut the hell up!" I harshly whispered through my teeth.

"Why I gotta shut the hell up? You wasn't shamed to let the dumb shit come out your mouth, so don't be shamed now." She rolled her eyes.

"Bitch, I'm not ashamed of shit," I said as I picked up a fry and threw it at her. "I just don't need you telling the whole fucking world about my plans to kill a bitch," I spat lowly, making sure only she could hear me.

I know what you're probably thinking right now, but listen, there's no way in hell I'm going to let the father of my children rot away in a damn jail cell all because his fucking wife, or lack thereof, is mad because he doesn't really want her ass.

If the shoe was on the other foot, I knew for a fact he wouldn't hesitate to do it for me. The proof was in the pudding of how he took care of Keymar's crazy unstable ass. Since he handled that for me without me having to ask, I felt it was only right I handled Carmilla for him.

"Just because you get dick from a killer, it doesn't make you one," Layla told me.

I just sucked my teeth as I waved her off. She was being very negative right now, and I didn't need that type of energy around me. Ever since Jacier left her, she had been walking around in a funk, being mean as hell to everyone and everything she crossed paths with.

"I didn't tell you my plans because I felt like I needed your permission. I'm grown as hell, so I'm going to do what I want regardless of what you say. I just told you because I felt, as my best friend, you would wanna to know," I said as I stood up.

I threw some money on the table to pay for our dinner before walking out of the restaurant. Even though I was seven months pregnant, I was still fairly small. At least that was what other people told me. Nobody could believe I was seven months along because I was carrying her so well. I was the same exact way when I was pregnant with Mateo.

"Bitch, I wish you would keep walking away from me. Don't think just because you pregnant you're invincible. I will slice and dice yo' ass all through this damn parking lot," Layla spat at me.

"You threatening me?" I asked as I stopped in my tracks, turning to look at her.

"No. I'm promising you that's what I'ma do," she said as she stuck her tongue out with her blade laying on it. "And if I was, what you gon' do? Kill me too?"

I sucked my teeth, trying to hide the smirk threatening to appear on my face. Layla was crazy as hell, and I blamed that shit on her brothers. The bitch stayed walking around with a weapon or two on her.

"Seriously though, Cherokee. Just think about this. Are you sure this is what you want to do? This is way different from us just beating a bitch's ass like we used to do back in the day. Once you cross that line, ain't no coming back. This might fuck with you for the rest of your life," Layla told me.

I nodded my head in understanding. Layla was putting her psychology degree to use. I understood where she was coming from 100 percent. Of course I had battled within myself on if this was the way I wanted to handle things. I was a fighter for sure, but murder? Hello no. Unfortunately, desperate times called for desperate measures.

"I get it, Lay. I'm sorry for blowing up on you in there. I'm just frustrated, but if you don't wanna help me, it's cool. I—"

"Bitch, I never said I wasn't going to help you." She rolled her eyes. "I just said make sure that you wanted to be a damn killer. You know I'm always down for whatever. But, if you hurt my goddaughter trying to be on some Kill Bill shit, I promise I'm going to kill you, then bring you back to life so Dillinger can kill you again. Now that's a threat," Layla said with her arms folded.

"Understood." I slowly nodded my head.

A smile crept on my face before we fell into a fit of laughter. No matter what crazy idea I presented to Layla, she was always with the shits. That was why she was my best friend.

* * *

"I AM SO UNCOMFORTABLE RIGHT NOW." I complained as I pulled at the bodysuit I had on.

Thanks to Colins, I had the info on where Carmilla had been staying. She was so big and bad in the courtroom but yet her scary ass had been hiding out ever since she gave up the info on Dillinger. She was so bold but yet she was in protective custody.

"Uhnt uhh, don't complain now, bitch. You the one who wanted to be out here on some die-hard type shit," Layla said as she cut her eyes at me.

"Shut up," was all I could say as we got out of the car.

It was a little after two in the morning, and we had just pulled up to the safe house Carmilla had been hiding out in. I looked around and didn't see any policemen around, which I thought was odd because Colin had assured me that she had around the clock twenty-four-hour security.

"I need to tell you something." Layla stopped me.

"What's wrong?" I asked.

"I called in some reinforcements."

I squinted my eyes at her and was about to say something real smart to her ass before the front door of the house came open, halting me.

"Can y'all bring y'all asses on in here so I can go? I got some pussy waiting on me. I ain't got all night to be playing with y'all," A'mir said as he stood on the porch smacking on whatever candy he just threw in his mouth.

"You so damn irritating," I told him, playfully mushing him as I made my way up the porch.

When I made it into the house, I stopped dead in the doorway when I saw the dead body of a man, who I assumed was an officer, laying on the ground with blood seeping from the bullet hole in the middle of his forehead. It felt as if everything I had eaten today was about to come up.

"Don't get scared now. You a stone-cold killer, ain't you?" A'mir laughed from behind me.

"Leave her the hell alone." Layla fussed at him after hitting him in the back of the head.

He just sucked his teeth before moving me out of the doorway so he could get in the house. Layla came in right behind him but stopped, turning to me with a look on her face.

"If you want to leave, we can. I can have them finish the job and get rid of her. It's completely up to you. Just say the word."

I wasn't even going to front; I definitely was thinking about turning my ass around and going the fuck home, but I had already come too far now.

"I'm good. Let's just go so I can get this shit over with," I told her.

She nodded her head as we followed the direction in which A'mir had just went in. The guys were in the den where they had Carmilla tied to a chair with duct tape over her mouth. When I walked in, her eyes got big as saucers before she rolled them.

"Hey, sexy." Amaad smiled.

"Hey, bae," I flirted back.

Since we were preteens, Amaad and I had always done some harmless flirting. I won't lie, Amaad has always been fine, but he and I never took it past flirting.

I smiled as I made my way over to Carmilla, snatching the duct tape off her mouth, causing her to let out a small yelp.

"This is very fucking pathetic of you. I hope you don't think you're actually going to get away with this?" she spat. "You know who my daddy is, and your ass will be under the damn jail."

She was trying to act tough, but I could see right through her little façade. She was scared shitless right now, as she should be.

"Remember what I told you, bitch. No talking," Layla told me.

"You right," I said before turning to her. "Let me see your gun."

Her face contorted into a frown before speaking. "Now what the hell would make you think I have a gun?" she asked as if she was confused about what I was asking.

"Why don't you have a gun, Lay?" I asked through a frustrated sigh.

"Why *would* I have a gun, Cherokee? This was your bright ass idea. Why don't *you* have a gun?" Layla threw back at me.

"You always got a damn weapon on you, so why would you pick now not to have a damn gun?"

"You—"

"Are y'all fucking serious right now?" A'mir exclaimed, cutting his sister off. "How the fuck y'all trying to kill some damn body with no fucking weapons? What the fuck y'all was gon' do if we wasn't here? Talk her to death? And you really thought this shit was a good idea?" he said to Akil, who just sat there shaking his head in shame while Amaad was chuckling.

Layla and I just stood there looking stupid while A'mir sucked his teeth and handed me his gun, mumbling something under his breath. I took the big ass gun from him, cocking it and aiming it right at her forehead.

"Bitch, you—"

Pff!

The bullet left the chamber silently before entering her skull, cutting her sentence off. I just stood there frozen, in utter disbelief that I had actually just killed something other than a damn bug. My hands were shaking as A'mir gently removed the gun from them.

"You okay?" he asked with a worried look on her face.

I went to answer him, but I couldn't. I quickly turned around, rushing out of the room. I ran back out of the front door, spilling my guts right there on the front yard.

I just killed her.

After I emptied my stomach, I started dry heaving. I couldn't stop, and I was suddenly starting to feel lightheaded.

"Aye, just calm down and take a deep breath. You gon' be okay," Akil said as he picked me up.

Against my will, tears started to roll down my face. I didn't see how people could just kill people like it was nothing. I thought I would feel relieved after killing Carmilla, but I was hyperventilating instead.

"You gotta breathe, girl. Don't put your daughter in stress like that." He fussed as he sat me down in the passenger seat.

He kneeled in front of me to help me calm down while Layla stood behind him looking worried.

"She okay, Boopy?" she asked her brother.

"Hell naw she ain't. She just did some shit that she knew she wasn't cut out for, but she'll be alright eventually. Just take her pregnant ass home so she can get some rest. Sleep might not be her best friend tonight, so I suggest you stay with her." Akil instructed his sister after assuring us that they would finish handling this situation for us.

She nodded her head in understanding before jumping in the driver's seat and pulling off. The duration of the ride was quiet, and I was happy about that. More so grateful for it. I didn't want to talk. I just wanted to get home and try to push tonight as far out of my mind as possible.

Dillinger

I couldn't walk out the doors of the fucking county fast enough. When they told me that the case was thrown out, I asked no questions. I didn't know how the shit happened, but please believe I was happy as hell to be free once again. With a smile on my face, I quickly made my way over to the awaiting car where Ms. Attitude stood with her arms folded.

"Wassup, girl? Why you looking like that?"

"You must not know how much you get on my nerves," she said, arms still folded.

"You acting like you not happy that I'm out."

"I'm not." Tashonda sucked her teeth as she walked to the driver's side, trying to hide her smile.

"Whatever, girl. You know you would've lost yo' damn mind if I had gotten locked up for the rest of my life."

She just rolled her eyes, opting out of coming back with a smart-ass comment because she knew it was true.

"Whatever. Just know you did not have to do that girl like that," Tashonda said lowly.

"I ain't do shit. I was locked up."

"Yeah, but you... you know what the hell I'm trying to say," she said as she popped me in my chest.

"On some real shit, Shonda, that was not my doing. I did not call for that shit to happen, and that's on my mama. I was shocked as hell when they told me that bitch was dead," I told her.

Even though I did want that bitch dead, I could honestly say I didn't put that hit out on her. They probably was thinking I had something to do with it, but they knew it wasn't me. I hadn't accepted any visits since before the trial started, and the only phone calls I made were to my son, which they recorded. I didn't write any letters, so they really didn't have shit on me, and that was why they had to let me go.

Carmilla was the prosecution's only hope of convicting me, and they knew without her, they didn't have a solid case. So major shout out to whoever took that problem off my hands. I may have wanted to do the shit myself, but the fact of the matter was she was taken care of.

"If not you, then who?" Tashonda asked in confusion.

"I don't know, but I'm not going to question God's plan," I let her know.

"Boy," she said, hitting me once again. "Don't put God in it. He ain't have nothing to do with that."

I just smirked as I laid my head back on the headrest. I had been confined for the past four months. At first, I wasn't worried because I knew they ain't have shit on me, but when I saw Carmilla walk into that courtroom, I just knew they were about to fry my black ass. I still couldn't believe she had the audacity to turn on me like that.

I couldn't front like I was the perfect nigga to Carmilla, but at least I did try. From day one, I tried to be the best nigga I could be for her. So much so that I hid what type of nigga that I was just to spare her, but in the end, she turned around and used that shit against me. She tried to paint the picture as if I was just some gruesome ass nigga that she feared oh so much.

"Hey," Tashonda said softly as she ran her hands through my wild hair. I snapped out of my thoughts, noticing that we were at my house. "What's on your mind?" she asked.

"Shit, everything," I told her.

"Everything happens for a reason, Dillinger. Maybe that was God's way of showing you people's true colors and helping you open your eyes to see who's really down for you. Now you know for a fact who will ride with you until the very end, no matter what. She called me faithfully to get updates on your trial, wondering if there was anything she could do to help. She truly loves you, and I don't even have to question if you love her. What y'all have is real love, and nothing or no one is worth losing that for, not even me. Do right by her, Dillinger," Tashonda told me before placing a soft kiss on my cheek.

"Thanks, Shonda. I really appreciate you, more than you'll ever know, and you already know I got you no matter what."

"You always have. Now get out of here and go be with your family. I know they're anxious to see you," she said with a smile.

Getting out of the car, I sighed in relief as I walked up to my front door. As soon as I let myself into the house, I was hit with the aroma of whatever was being cooked.

"Yo, Cherry!" I called out to her.

Scratching my head, I walked to the kitchen where I got a big shock.

"Surprise!" everyone yelled.

Of course, Cherokee had thrown together a little shindig to welcome a nigga home. Everyone I considered family was here. Layla, Akil, A'mir, Amaad, and even my baby Reign was here. Cherokee walked over to me with the biggest smile I had ever seen.

"Welcome home," she gushed.

"Thank you, baby," I said as I pulled her into me, placing a kiss on her lips while gripping her ass in my hands.

"Eww." Mateo frowned up, making everybody laugh.

"Y'all acting like this nigga did a ten-year bid or something. His ass was only in the county," I heard from behind me.

"Get the fuck outta here!" I exclaimed through laughter as I pulled Santos in for a brotherly hug.

This one right here was truly a big surprise. I had no idea my right-hand man was out of his coma, let alone out of the damn hospital. If I was a crying ass nigga, tears of joy would definitely be flowing down my face right about now.

"Okay, y'all. This is a lovely moment and all, but can we eat now? This little girl is hungry," Cherokee said as she pointed to her small, round stomach.

"Is she hungry, or is her greedy ass mama hungry?" Layla asked, causing everyone to laugh.

"Both," Cherokee answered while simultaneously flicking Layla off. "You go sit down somewhere. I'll fix your plate," she said as she turned to go toward the food.

I gently grabbed her hand to stop her. She looked up at me with a questioning look as I pulled her closer to me. I unconsciously licked my lips as I peered down at her. After four long ass months, it felt good as fuck to be holding her again. I placed my massive hand on her stomach, gaining a smile from her.

"Nah, you go sit yo' lil ass down somewhere and let me fix the plates. I'm home now, so all this ripping and running shit you been doing is dead," I let her know.

"Dilly, I—"

"It wasn't up for a debate."

"Okay," was all she said as she placed a kiss on my lips before going to sit down like I told her to.

A few hours later, everyone was full and slightly tipsy, for those of us who could drink. Layla, Cherokee, A'mir, and Amaad were now in an intense shit talking game of spades. The kids were in the playroom that Cherokee had set up for them, and everyone was just having a good time overall. I took this as the perfect opportunity to go talk to my right-hand man.

I found him and Akil on the back porch, talking and passing a blunt back and forth between each other.

"What y'all girl scouts back here gossiping about?" I asked as I stepped out the patio door.

"Yo soft ass," Akil cracked. "Wassup though? How it feel to be back out here?" he asked.

"Shit, you know better than anybody how it feel to be free, and my lil' ass stint wasn't shit compared to what you did. But on the real, I wanna thank you for what you did. I was confused as shit at first, but now that I see you here, it all makes sense to me now," I told Santos just as he hit the blunt.

He blew the smoke out his mouth while giving me crazy ass look. "Fuck is you talking about?" he asked in confusion.

"You know what I'm talking about, nigga. Handling Carmilla for me."

"Hold up, you think I did that shit? You know how we rock, and you know damn well I definitely would've handled that shit for you, but that wasn't my doing," Santos informed me.

I furrowed my brows in confusion as I looked over at Akil, but he just shook his head to let me know that it wasn't him either.

"That wasn't us," Akil told me.

Now I was really confused. Fuck confused; a nigga was flabbergasted by this news. I was really standing there racking my brain, trying to figure out who the hell else it could've been, when Santos started laughing.

"Get the fuck outta here." He continued to laugh. "Nah, that can't be it," he said.

"What, nigga? Let me know something," I told him.

He was too busy looking behind me like he was really amazed, so I turned around to see what he was looking at. I followed his line of vision, and to my damn surprise, he was looking right dead at Cherokee. I didn't even have to ask him what the hell he was talking about because the shit hit me like a ton of bricks.

I stormed off back toward the house, leaving them two just

standing there. When I got back into the house, I walked over to Cherokee, getting real close to her ear.

"Let me holla at you real quick," I said before grabbing her arm.

It was as if everything came to a halt. Gone was the loudness and laughter. Now everyone sat around the table quietly with looks of worry on their faces as I damn near pulled her ass away from everyone.

"Dillinger, why—"

"What the fuck did you do?" I asked through my teeth as I lightly grabbed her throat.

I ignored the terrified look in her eyes as I backed her up against the wall. I didn't apply too much pressure because she was pregnant, and my daughter was the only reason I wasn't going to fuck her up right now.

"What the fuck did you do, Cherokee?" I reiterated but a little louder this time.

"I got you off on a murder charge and brought you home," she said as best as she could considering I had a grip on her throat.

"Bi—are you fucking crazy! Why the fuck would you do some dumb ass shit like that?"

By now, tears had formed in her eyes, and I was too pissed off to give a fuck right now.

"Let me go." She cried as she clawed at my hand.

"Let her go, Dillinger! She's pregnant. What the fuck is wrong with you!" Layla yelled as she tried to come help her friend.

"This ain't got shit to do with you, Lay. Take yo' ass on somewhere," I said through gritted teeth.

"I don't give a fuck who it got to do with, but I know you better remove yo' fuckin' hand from her throat, and I'm not gon' say it no more," she spat.

I ignored her as I continued to look down at Cherokee in rage. I couldn't believe she really thought the shit she did was okay.

"Ahh, fuck!" I cried out at the pain in my hand.

I looked down at the blood on my hand before looking up at Layla like she had lost her fucking mind. Her crazy ass really just stood there and sliced my fucking hand with her razor.

"What the fuck is y'all doing?" I heard.

By now, everyone was standing in the hallway looking at us.

"This nigga was choking her, so I cut his ass." Layla smacked her lips.

"Get the fuck out my house, Cherokee."

"What?" she asked with a look of hurt.

"Get the fuck out," I said slowly so she could see that I wasn't playing with her.

"Come on, nigga. You tripping," Santos said.

Cherokee just stood there in disbelief before Layla grabbed her hand, mumbling something along the lines of 'fuck that nigga'. Never in my life had I ever put my hands on Cherokee, so the fact that she even pissed me off to that point meant that we needed to be as far away from each other as possible right now.

Maybe I overacted a little, but the fact that the mother of my children actually killed someone wasn't sitting right with me. Why would she ever think something like that was okay to do? She was surrounded by all these niggas who were certified killers, but instead of using them to handle the situation, she'd rather have caught a body her damn self. Then to top it off, these niggas knew about it but didn't think it was a good idea to stop her.

6

Jacier

I laid my head back on the plush couch while exhaling a cloud of smoke. I was currently at the club with my brother and some niggas I grew up with. I honestly didn't want to be here, but I was damn near begged to come out, so I was here, trying to make the best of it.

"Here," Jacieon said as he tried to hand me his Styrofoam cup.

"Naw, I'm straight." I shook my head.

One thing I didn't fuck around with was that lean bullshit. That was just one craze I couldn't get with. Niggas would try anything to get high. The shit was ridiculous. They were just one step away from being full-blown crackheads if you asked me. I was good with my weed. My bitch Mary Jane ain't never let me down.

"Nigga, you need to do something. You killing my fucking vibe!" My brother yelled over the music.

I just waved him and his bullshit off. "Nigga, you should've just let me stay my ass at the crib, then you wouldn't have to worry about," I reminded him.

"Nigga, I was tryna do yo' love sick ass a fucking favor. I keep telling you bitches come a dime a dozen. Fuck is you moping around for, Trouble? All this pussy in the building and you wanna be in here sulking and shit." Jacieon rambled on about nothing.

I just sucked my teeth as I got up from the couch I was sitting on. Everybody around me was turned up, and then here go my sorry ass. As I made my way to the bathroom, I pulled out my phone to check up on my baby girl. I would much rather be at home cuddling up with her, but whatever.

Me: *Y'all good? Need me to come home?*

After sending the text, I made my way to the bathroom to relieve myself. After handling my business, I made my way over to the sink to wash my hands. I just stood there looking in the mirror. I really had to shake this shit off. Layla's ass had my head so fucked up that it ain't make no fucking sense.

No matter what I did, I couldn't shake her. It had been weeks since I talked to her or heard her voice. Every time I get the yearning to call her, my pride wouldn't allow me to do it. To say I didn't feel some type of way about the way shit played out would be me lying. The only thing I ever asked Layla to do was keep it a hunnid with me.

It wasn't even the fact that she was going to see the nigga. It was the fact that she called herself being sneaky about the shit. All she had to do was let me know that she wanted to visit the nigga, and I would've been cool on it. But the fact that she was doing the shit behind my back on some slick shit had me feeling like I couldn't trust her.

After the last female I dealt with, I was being very cautious. I was taking a leap of faith by even wanting to be with Layla because my trust was beyond fucked up. Still, I tried to make something work with her, and I feel like the shit came back to slap me in the face.

I don't care what anybody said, Layla still had feelings for that nigga. I mean, how could she not after they had a been together for so long? It's not that easy to get over someone you really were in love with, no matter how bad they hurt you, and I was saying that shit from experience.

The vibration in my pocket snapped me out of my thoughts. Getting it together, I made my way out of the bathroom while removing my phone from my pocket.

Nova: *Boy, ain't you supposed to be enjoying your night? She's good, I'm good. We're good. Leave me alone.*

I couldn't do shit but chuckle. I swear that smart mouth ass girl was my fucking world. It wasn't shit in this world that I wouldn't do for my fucking sister. I wasn't even going to text her back, because I knew there was no point. She wouldn't reply anyway.

"Damn, my bad."

I was so deep into my phone that I accidentally collided with someone, dropping my phone. I bent down to pick it up, but when I stood back up, it was as if the earth stood still. She stood there frozen like she was afraid to move. I felt as my top lip curled up and my temper rising.

"Fuck up out my way." I snarled.

As I moved around her, she reached out and touched my hand.

"Jacier, wait! I'm sorry."

I snatched my hand away before walking so close up on her that you would've thought I was going to kiss her ass. She was so scared that she jumped back, but I got even closer, trapping her between my body and the wall.

"Sorry? Bitch, sorry?" I had never been the type to disrespect a woman, but Danielle wasn't a woman; she was a snake. "You fucked that nigga behind my back, had a baby by him, then had the fucking audacity to try and pin the baby on me, and all you can fucking say is you sorry?"

I was so pissed that my chest was heaving up and down. The bitch standing before me had betrayed me in the worst way possible. It wasn't shit in this world she couldn't have gotten from me. I thought she was going to really be the one to carry my last name. My dumb ass was really in love with her, but it took me four years to see her true colors.

While I was at the hospital grieving the loss of my best friend, Nyomi, this bitch was riding another nigga's dick. Not just any nigga though, but a nigga I considered a brother. A nigga that ate meals at my mama's house when his daddy was nowhere to be found, and his mama was too strung out to remember she even had a child. A nigga that I would've gave my last to. A nigga that I had been in plenty of shoot outs with. A nigga that I came from nothing with. A nigga I broke bread with. A nigga who snaked me all for some pussy.

Danielle had the nerve to be standing here looking at me as if she was hurt, like I wasn't the one who was betrayed. It had been some months since the last time I'd seen her, and it was taking everything in me not to snap her fucking neck. Nyomi tried to tell me about her ass, but I was too gone in the head to listen to her. If only she was here now to see how this shit played out in the end.

"Jacier, please, it wasn't like that—"

"I don't give a fuck what it was like. Stay the fuck away from me, Danielle. Ain't no telling how I'll react the next time I see you," I spat before turning to walk away.

As if I wasn't in the mood already, I definitely was ready to get the fuck on now. I didn't even bother to go back up to VIP. I was so pissed off right now, and being around all these people wasn't going to make the shit no better.

I just used the back door to exit the club. I didn't even bother to tell Jacieon I was gone so I already knew I was going to hear his mouth tomorrow. Even though he was my big brother, that nigga swore he was my daddy sometimes. I knew it was coming from a good place, but the shit irritated me because I was grown as fuck and didn't need a babysitter.

Jumping in my car, I sped out of the parking lot, burning rubber in the process. Now I was really regretting the fact that I didn't stay my ass at home. So now I didn't just have Layla fucking with my mental, but it was Danielle as well, once again.

I gotta get these women off my mind.

34

It took me about twenty-five minutes to get to the home I used to own, which now belonged to my sister. Using my key, I quickly let myself in before setting the alarm and making my way to go check on my girls. I stopped by Nyami's room, and of course my baby girl was knocked out in her crib. I leaned down to kiss her on her forehead, leaving her room just as quietly as I walked in.

Nova's bedroom door was cracked open, so I went to check on her as well. She was laying under the covers in the middle of her bed, watching a movie. When I stepped in the room, she sat up in her bed until she realized it was me.

"Jacier? Don't be scaring me like that, boy. I thought I told you we were good," she fussed.

I sighed deeply as I walked over to her bed. I lay at the feet of her bed on my back, just staring up at the dark ceiling.

"What's wrong?" she asked.

"Am I a bad person?" I asked, answering her question with a question of my own.

"Just because you make some bad choices in life, it doesn't make you a bad person. Why are you asking me that?"

"Just wondering why I keep getting fucked over," I stated.

"When you have a big heart, it's easy for you to get hurt, but that's not your fault. Does this have anything to do with the situation with Layla?" she asked.

"No. Well, partially. I seen her tonight... Danielle," I told my sister.

If nobody knew how fucked up I was behind the shit Danielle's no good ass pulled, my little sister knew. She was so pissed off that she actually went looking for Danielle to beat her ass, but she was too scared to come out and fight Nova. Now, my little sister was honestly the sweetest person you could ever meet, so you knew the shit had to be bad if she was ready to fight.

Nobody in this world knew me like my sister. She was literally my human diary. We had been through so much shit together that you couldn't even imagine. For some reason, my brother only saw me as Trouble, the menace to society I was labeled as. With Nova though, I was just regular ass Jacier, her big brother, protector, and biggest supporter.

"Come here." She ushered me over to her while reaching over on her nightstand for one of her essential oils. "So how did you react?" she asked as she gently massaged my head.

"Calmer than I should have. I accidentally bumped into her, but when I realized who she was, I instantly felt rage. Her stupid ass had the nerve to spew some bullshit about how she was sorry. She better be glad I'm not the type to put my hands on a woman, because I really wanted to rip her head off her fucking shoulders," I vented.

"First of all, that bitch is bold as hell. She knows damn well she's not sorry, simply because she fucked him more than once. Honestly though, Jacier, you need to forgive her," Nova said.

I quickly sat up and looked at my sister like she had lost her rabid ass mind.

"Let me clean my ear out because I know I couldn't have heard you say what the fuck I think I heard you say," I told her as I put my finger in my ear to clean out the wax.

"You are so extra that it don't make no sense. Lay back and hear me out," she said.

"Naw, I'm good. I don't wanna hear that shit." I shook my head.

"Have I ever steered you wrong? Have I ever told you something that was absolutely absurd?" she asked. I just shook my head because she honestly had never led me astray. "Then lay your big head ass back so I can help you not be so tense and you can hear what I have to say," Nova demanded.

Smacking my lips, I opted out of speaking as I did what I was told to do.

"Like I was saying, you need to forgive her, not for her, but for you. You're cutting your own blessings off by harboring around all those ill feelings you have for her. I know it sounds dumb, and trust me, I know exactly how hard it is to forgive someone who's not sorry, but you have to. The moment you forgive someone who has wronged you, you will have peace in your life. Have you ever stopped to wonder why things didn't work out with Layla the way you wanted them to? It wasn't all on her; it was you too," she informed me.

"How? That shit with Layla had nothing to do with me," I said, getting slightly defensive.

"You got mad at her and left her because you thought she was doing some bullshit behind your back. Granted, she should've told you she was going to visit him, but the man was in a coma, Jacier. It's not like she was sneaking off to go have sex with him. You said it yourself that you didn't mind if they remained friends. That was part of her being a friend. Just like you have a big heart, so does Layla. So are you honestly going to tell me that the way you reacted didn't in the slightest way have anything to do with what you went through with Danielle? You have to forgive her, Jacier. Cleanse your life and your soul of all that negativity," Nova told me.

To be so young, I swear my little was so wise. Everything she was saying actually made perfect sense like always. I could be stubborn sometimes, and even though she was right about everything she was saying, I felt like Danielle didn't deserve my forgiveness. It was an uphill battle, but I would take into consideration everything she just said.

7

Layla

"*H*ey, Ms. Layla. These just came for you," one of my boys said as he walked into my office holding a bouquet of flowers and an edible arrangement.

"Thank you, sweetheart," I said as I took the items from him.

I didn't even have to wonder who sent them because I already knew. I pulled a small card out the flowers and read it.

Thinking of you, hope you've been well

Ever since he left me, Jacier would still spontaneously send me flowers or some food item to my job. It had been a little over a month since we broke up, and this was the only way we communicated with each other. Nova called to check on me regularly and even FaceTimed me so I could see Nyami's little cute self. She and I had formed a bond after Jacier got shot, so she told me that no matter what her brother and I went through, she wanted us to remain close.

She would always have me confirm that I got the items that her brother sent, so I sent her text to let her know I received the flowers and the fruit. It hurt me that this was what Jacier and I had been reduced to because we both were too stubborn to reach out to each other. On the flip side, it warmed my heart to know that he still cared enough to even do things for me.

My phone vibrated on my desk, so I picked it up, expecting to get a smart mouthed response from Nova about how her brother and I was bringing down her energy or something along those lines, but instead, it was a text from Santos. I wasn't surprised that he texted me either. He had been hitting me up a lot to check on me. I guess Cherokee had accidentally slipped up and told him about how I came to visit him every day he was in the hospital. Since then, he had been reaching out to me every day.

Santos: *You busy? I'm outside and just wanted to talk to you.*

I raised my brow as I read his text. Since I started working here years ago, Santos had never been to my job. I didn't even know he was aware of where I worked.

Me: *Sure, I'm on my way out.*

Picking a grape off my edible arrangement, I threw it in my mouth before locking up my office to see exactly what this man could want that he came all the way to my job to talk to me. When I got outside, Santos was parked right in front.

"What's up?" I asked as I walked over to his window.

"Man, get yo' ass in. It's hot as fuck, and you letting out all my cool air because yo' ass wanna be stubborn," he said as he rolled his window up while simultaneously hitting his locks.

I smacked my lips but did as I was told as I walked over to the other side of his truck to get in. I wasn't going to act like it wasn't hot as hell in this damn Miami heat. I sighed in relief once I got in his truck and the cold air hit my skin.

"What can I do for you, Rahiem?" I asked.

"Damn, so I'm Rahiem now?" he asked.

"I'm confused. Is that not the name on your birth certificate?" I asked.

"Yeah. I'm just used to you only calling me that when you're mad at me," Santos said.

"I mean, we aren't actually on the best of terms right now so... yeah."

"But we were on good enough terms for you to come see me every day and for you to love on my child?" he said like he was confused about something.

I sighed heavily because we were only sixty seconds into the conversation, and I was already regretting coming out here to talk to him. Whenever I was around him for more than two seconds, he was always letting something smart fly out of his mouth just to irritate the hell out of me.

"Reign is innocent. I'm a grown ass woman who would never resent a child for the mistakes her parents made. She's a joy to be around, and she's marked her spot on my heart. As for you, I was just doing what I hoped you would've done for me. That doesn't change the way I feel about you or what you did," I let him know.

"What about you though, Lay?"

"What about me?" I questioned.

"You love throwing up in my face what I did but don't ever speak on the fact that you was hiding shit from me too. If you're gonna crucify me, you might as well build your cross and put it up next to mine," Santos spat.

I just looked at him through squinted eyes, slightly amused about the fact that he was trying to turn this around on me.

"I'm not about to do this with you," I said as I reached for the door handle to get out.

Of course, Santos wasn't going to let me just walk away, so he hit the locks, locking me in the car. I hit the locks to unlock it, but he quickly locked the doors again. At that point, I just gave up because I knew we could go at it all day.

"Crazy how people forget that when you point your finger, you have three more pointing back at you," he said.

"You're stupid. What I did wasn't shit compared to what you did. I didn't have a baby on you. We were already broken up when I got pregnant, and I killed my child because of *you*. I killed my chances of ever being a mother just for you to turn around and get another bitch pregnant and hide it from me for two years. Two fucking years, Rahiem!" I yelled.

I hadn't even realized I was crying until I felt the tears falling from my face. I thought I was getting over it, but I clearly was wrong. I loved Reign; honestly, I did, but every time I looked at her, she was a reminder of my failure as a woman.

I had literally been to hell and back with this nigga. Was a shoulder for him to cry on, was his peace whenever he was going through shit in the streets, cooked, cleaned, and fucked on demand, but yet, that still wasn't good enough to keep him from straying.

Even after I found out he cheated on me, my heart still yearned for him. So much so that I had the audacity to put my happiness on the back burner for him when I found out I had gotten pregnant by another man. I wanted to spare his feelings and not hurt him, so much so that I was willing to hurt myself.

I just sat there breathing hard before I had enough of this. I vowed that these would be the last fucking tears I let fall over this whole ordeal. I couldn't go back and change the past, so there was no reason to keep dwelling over it and crying over spilled milk.

I reached for the lock, hitting it, but once again, Santos wouldn't let me out.

"Stop playing with me," I said.

"Layla—"

"Stop fucking talking to me and let me out this fucking car! Now!" I yelled at him.

I didn't know why this man refused to catch the hint and leave me the fuck alone. He had already succeeded in crushing my heart. What the fuck was he gunning for next? My soul?

"A'Layla, you can scream, yell, hit me, whatever you need to do that will help you let it all out. You may not believe me, but I truly am sorry from the bottom of my fucking heart. Since we've been apart, I feel like I lost my fucking best friend. You was there when I had nobody and nothing. You loved me when I was out here bumming. You never judged me but loved me for who I was. I don't regret my daughter, but I do deeply regret the pain I inflicted on you. I'm not going to let up, because I'm too invested into this shit. I know you're upset right now, but I'll call you in a few days with plans for us," Santos said as he hit his locks to let me out.

I didn't even bother to respond as I jumped out of his truck and quickly made my way back into my job. Suddenly, I started to feel exhausted, physically and mentally. It had been a minute since I had a vacation, and I definitely felt one coming, even if I had to go by myself. This was starting to be just a little too much for me. How was I single but going through relationship problems with not one but two niggas?

8

Cherokee

*A*s I pulled up to my house, I rolled my eyes in annoyance at the truck that was parked in my driveway. I hadn't spoken to Dillinger since the day he came home and blew up on me. That was weeks ago. He hadn't tried to reach out to me and vice versa. At this point, I honestly was over the whole situation. I was eight months pregnant and didn't have the energy to be playing with this man.

"Don't even think about going anywhere near that game until your homework is done, and I'm not playing with you," I told Mateo as I let us in the house.

"I hear you." He mumbled before speaking to his dad.

I ignored Dillinger sitting on my couch as I made my way to my room. I was hot, tired, irritated, pregnant, and most importantly not in the mood for him or his shit. I peeled my dress from my body before lying on my bed. I wanted to take a quick nap before I got tonight's dinner started.

"Cherry," Dillinger said softly as he called himself trying to ease in the bed behind me.

"Go the hell away, Dillinger Rivera. I don't have nothing to say to you." I mumbled while closing my eyes.

Ignoring everything I just said, he climbed in the bed, burying his face in my neck. I was about to push him off of me when I felt something moist. Instantly, I sat up and looked at him with wide eyes. This man was literally sitting over here crying. Now I was on high alert because the last time I saw this man cry was when he lost his mom. That was the first as well as the last time I saw a tear fall from Dillinger Rivera's eyes.

"What's wrong?" I asked, full of concern.

I didn't know what type of voodoo this man had over me to make me switch emotions like that. Literally two seconds ago, I wanted nothing to do with him, but now I was worried about him and wanted to make sure he was okay.

"I fucked up. I fucked up real bad," he said.

"What are you talking about, Dillinger? How did you fuck up?"

"I did something I said I would never do, and that's disrespect you. Not only that, but I was stupid enough to put my hands on you while you're carrying my daughter. I always said that a nigga who put his hands on women was less of a man. I'm so sorry, especially since I know what you've been through in the past. I honestly wasn't mad at you for what you did. I was just pissed that I even put you in that predicament to feel as if you even had to kill for me. I've always looked at you as my good girl, and now I tainted you."

These damn pregnancy hormones were getting to me, as I sat here crying right along with his ass. I knew Dillinger would be mad when he found out what I had done. He just went a little bit farther than I expected him to when he choked me. Granted, he didn't hurt me, but still, the fact of the matter was he did it.

Just from the fact that he was really sitting here crying let me know just how sorry he was. Dillinger was not an emotional person, especially when it came to crying, so I knew he was serious right now.

"Dillinger—"

"Let's get married." He cut me off.

"Wait, what did you just say?" I asked, confused.

"You heard me. Let's go get married," he said as he reached in his pocket, coming out with a ring box.

He can't be serious right now.

I'd be damned if he wasn't serious as hell right now. The diamonds in the ring he had just presented me with were definitely dancing. I sat on the bed with my mouth agape because I honestly didn't know what to say.

"But—"

"Nah, no buts. Fuck what anyone would say or how muthufuckas would feel. Let me make this right and do what I should've done. I told you that morning that it should've been you I was marrying. I'm tired of being in that big ass house without you and my son. You're about to have my daughter, and I want to make an honest woman out of you before she gets here. I don't want you to just be the mother of my children. I want you to be Mrs. Rivera. The *real* Mrs. Rivera. I already lost you for eight years. I'm not trying to lose you ever again," Dillinger said.

It was beautiful as hell, I admit that, but I didn't know if Dillinger and I were ready for that right now. This was a huge step for us. Granted, we'd known each other for forever, but marriage was a different ball game. Not to mention, he was already married just last week until I killed his wife.

"Damn," he said as he stood up from the bed, looking as if I had just punched him in the face. "You don't want to marry me," he said more as a statement than a question.

"It's not that I don't want to. I'm just not trying to jump head first into something all because you feel bad about a fight that happened between us. Getting married is not going to solve any of our problems right now, Dillinger, and to be honest, it might actually make things worse," I told him.

He didn't bother to respond verbally, but he did nod his head up in down as if he was acknowledging what I said. He slid the ring box back into his pocket before turning around, walking out of my room.

I sighed deeply before lying back on the bed just staring up at the ceiling. This was all beginning to be a little too much for me.

Reaching over for my purse, I grabbed my phone to text my best friend.

Me: *I'm stressed and need a drink. At this point I don't care if it has alcohol in it.*

Almost instantly, she had text me back.

Layla: *Same. My house tomorrow?*

Me: *I'll be there.*

After confirming my plans with Layla, I threw the phone to the side and covered my face with my arm. I was so exhausted that it didn't take long for sleep to consume me.

* * *

"BITCH, YOU SAID NO?" Layla exclaimed through laughter.

I had just finished telling her about what had taken place yesterday between Dillinger and me. I still couldn't believe that man had the nerve to ask me to marry him all out the blue like that.

"Shut up, Lay. It's not funny," I told her as I tried to hide my smile.

"The hell if it ain't. I never thought I would ever see the day you told that man no, but to turn down his proposal? You are a bad bitch for that one. I just can't believe it."

"Well believe it. I don't know how he thought I was going to just say yes, especially after his last little stunt."

"So you'll have another baby by him but not marry him?" Layla asked me with her face twisted into a frown.

Whether she knew it or not, I definitely felt the sting of her words. Regardless of if I married him or not, I would still have to deal with

Dillinger for the rest of my life just based off the fact that we had kids together. Either way, I was dumb as hell.

"Would you take Santos back if he walked in here right now with a ring and said he wanted to marry you?" I asked.

"Santos ain't no 'let's get married' type of nigga, and we're not talking about me right now. We're talking about you." She rolled her eyes.

Maybe she thought I wasn't going to catch on, but I noticed how she just danced around and avoided my question. I wasn't going to call her out on it just yet because we were in fact talking about me.

"He cheated on me—"

"That was nine years ago, Cherokee."

"It doesn't matter—he did it. Not only that, but he married another woman after professing his love for me the night before. My son was kidnapped because of him, he killed my only sister, and choked me out after I killed a bitch just so he could be a free man. All of that, and I'm supposed to just forgive him and marry him like none of this shit ever happened?" I asked, really confused.

"Wait, killed your sister? Dillinger killed Keila?"

I forgot I hadn't told her the truth about Keila's death. She was there in the hospital with me when the detectives informed me that she was dead, but I had never told her that I confronted Dillinger about it, and he admitted to killing my sister in not so many words.

I just gave her a look that answered her question without me actually having to open my mouth and say it.

"Damn, I didn't know that, but you have to do what's best for you, Cherokee. If you don't think marrying him is the right thing to do, then by no means, please don't do it. On the other hand, if that's what you want but you're afraid of how it will be accepted, fuck that. It's your life, and can't nobody tell you how to live it but you. Every relationship goes through shit, especially when y'all have been together that long, eight-year break or not. If y'all really want it to work, it will. Just know that whatever decision you make, I'm behind you all the way," Layla told me.

I just sat back in the seat and rubbed my stomach where my baby girl was kicking. A small smile spread across my face as I looked at Layla.

"I guess the same applies to you too, Lay. Your ass is in a love triangle, whether you want to admit it or not. If your heart is screaming for Santos, then work it out with him. If it's yearning for Jacier, work it out with him. Hell, if you want to be a city girl and not give a fuck about a nigga, then I'm down with that too. I'm not going to be pregnant for too much longer." I smiled.

My best friend just looked up at me with a sad smile, but she opted out of speaking on the matter. My baby was conflicted. She had two sexy ass men out here trying to prove their love for her. I wish that was the only problem I had in my life.

9

Santos

*a*fter reaching up to knock on the door, I nervously stuffed my hands in my pocket as I waited for an answer. A few moments later, the door opened, and I bullshit you not, I fell in love all over again.

"Hey," I said breathlessly.

"Hello, Rahiem," Layla said as she gave me a small smile.

Yup, you read it right. Ya boy finally did it. I finally got Layla to agree to go out with me. All I asked her for was one date, and if she honestly could say that she still didn't feel anything for the kid, I would leave her alone for good. Or, at least *try* to leave her alone for good.

"You look beautiful," I told her as I let my eyes roam over her.

She was dressed simply in a red strapless shirt that looked good against her chocolate skin, some jeans that looked as if they were painted on, along with some red heels that had her manicured toes looking real suckable.

She reached up and fixed the collar on my Polo shirt. "Thanks; not too shabby yourself," she said before turning to lock her door.

I couldn't help but to lick my lips at the way her ass was sitting in the jeans she was wearing. I hadn't slid up in anything since I'd been out of my coma, and if I played my cards right, I would be fucking the shit out of Layla by the end of the night.

"You ready?" she asked, snapping me out of my thoughts of fucking her from the back.

"Hell yeah," I said as I turned around and led up to my car.

When we got to the car, Layla stood there with her arms folded while I walked over to the driver's side and jumped in. I sat there for a moment confused about what the hell she was doing, until the shit hit me. I jumped out of the car and quickly rushed over to where she was standing as she watched me closely with a raised brow.

"My bad, bae." I laughed it off as I opened the car door for her.

"Thanks." She mumbled as she got in.

Get it together, nigga.

When I got back in the car, I picked up the aux cord, handing it over to her.

"I'll even be okay with you playing all that sap ass girly shit you like listening to," I told her.

She cut her eyes at me before chuckling and taking the cord from me.

"Who knew you could be so romantic," Layla said with her voice dripping with nothing but sarcasm.

I just shrugged it off and didn't say nothing, because there wasn't really shit I could say. This was literally the first date I had ever been on, despite Layla and I being together for years. A nigga was only four-teen when Layla and I got together, so dates wasn't big on the priority list back then. Even throughout the years, she never had pressed me to take her out on a date. Looking back at it now, that probably was some sorry ass shit on my part. Layla definitely deserved to be taken out, and not to mention, she was bad as fuck, so I certainly should have been showing her off to the world.

Reaching over, I turned the music a little so she could hear me.

"So how was your day today? How was work and shit?" I asked.

"Fine," she said slowly, not bothering to go into detail about her day.

"Damn, Lay. You acting like this our first date or something. Loosen the hell up. What you so uptight for?"

"This is our first date," she threw back at me.

"Okay. Well you acting like you don't know me or like you ain't never been around me before," I told her.

"I don't know you, because the Santos I know never planned dates. Just because you've known a person for years doesn't mean you really know them," Layla said, taking shots at me.

I let out a loud groan before yelling at the top of my lungs. I gripped the steering wheel with my left hand before looking over at Layla while simultaneously pressing down on the pedal.

"I will kill both of us in this bitch," I told her.

"Do it," Layla said.

The look she gave me let me know that she was daring me to crash into something. A smile crept across my face slowly as I took some pressure off the pedal, slowing the car down.

"Damn, I love yo' crazy ass." I smiled while putting my eyes back on the road.

She knew I wasn't going to do anything that would cause her any harm. I reached over to turn the music back up for the duration of the ride, but she turned it back down, turning in her seat so that she was looking at me.

"What's up?" I asked.

"Why did you do it? Why did you shoot Jacier?" Layla asked, catching me off guard.

"I'm not about to sit up here and discuss this nigga with you. Fuck him," I spat.

She folded her arms over her chest and gave me a look that let me know that she wasn't playing with me. I didn't do nothing but wave her off because I was not about to do this with her little ass. Out the corner of my eye, I could see her reaching in her purse, and I knew shit was about to get real.

"Aye, listen. I'm not Dillinger, so if you think you about to just sit up here and slice and dice my ass up, you got another fucking thing coming. You definitely ain't have to do my boy like that." I shook my head.

"Rahiem Jakim Santos, stop playing with me and let's be real. How do you expect me to consider us being together again if you're going to continue to keep shit from me?"

I sighed before licking my lips. I hated the fact that her ass knew just what to say to get me going. "Aight. Since you wanna know so fucking much, I did it because he had something that belonged to me. He had you. I had already told you that I would kill any nigga that you thought you were going to move on with. You thought the shit was a joke so I had to show you just how funny I can be," I let her know with a shrug.

Not one ounce of me feels bad about what I did. Anybody who knew me or even knew of me knows for a fact that I don't play when it comes to Layla. Yea, we have our shit to us but at the end of the day, I'm not going to sit back and let her be with somebody else.

"You don't fucking own me, Rahiem. That was so fucked up and asinine of you to do. You should've shot your damn self for sticking your dick in a bitch, getting her pregnant, then hiding it." She rolled her eyes.

Before I could say anything else, her phone started ringing loud as hell in the car since it was still hooked up to the aux cord.

"Hello—"

"Layla! Ughhh!" Cherokee yelled through the phone, putting Layla and I both on alert.

"What's wrong, Cherokee?"

"I fell in the shower, and I'm having unbearable pains in my stomach. I know you're on your date with Santos—ahhh... but nobody is home but me, and I can't get in touch with Dillinger." Cherokee cried.

"We're on our way," I said.

"No, no, no! The ambulance is on the way to get me. Can you please just try to get in touch with your friend. He had Mateo with him," Cherokee informed me.

"Okay. I'm about to call him right now. We'll meet you at the hospital," I let her know as I pulled out my phone while busting an illegal U-turn in traffic.

"You guys are on a date, I'll—"

"I said we'll meet you their girl, now hush." I cut her off as I texted Dillinger our emergency code on his business line.

I knew that if we couldn't reach him on his personal phone, he always answered his business phone, no matter what. Just as I knew he would, he called me from his business line.

"What—"

"Nigga, get to the hospital now! Cherokee fell in the shower, and the ambulance on the way to get her. She said she been calling you but can't reach you," I told him, skipping all formalities.

"Fuck, man! My phone dead, but good looking." He hung up before I could say anything else.

This wasn't how the fuck I planned my date night with Layla to go, but Cherokee was family, and I had to make sure she and my niece were straight.

Dillinger

estiny Mylah Rivera. My baby girl came into this world weighing five pounds and seven ounces. She had a hair full of curly locs like her daddy and was one of the most beautiful things I'd ever seen. I had never seen a baby be born before, and I swear it was life changing for me. Not that I didn't respect her before, but Cherry definitely had my respect after I witnessed everything she had to endure to bring my baby girl into this world.

"Aye, Cherry, you okay?" I asked as I held our baby girl.

I knew child birth took a lot out of you and you be tired as fuck afterwards, but she wasn't looking too good right now. She was looking pale as hell and was just lying there. Layla jumped up from her seat and rushed over to Cherokee just as the monitor they had her hooked up to started going crazy.

Next thing I knew, I heard all types of codes being yelled while nurses rushed into the room. They asked us to step out of the room, but I wasn't budging. She was literally just up and alert while smiling at our daughter, but now she was in a crisis. There was no way in hell I was leaving her in here like that when I knew she needed me.

"Sir, we—"

"I'm not fucking leaving!" I barked at the bitch that was in my face.

Destiny started to whine in my arms, and that was when Layla walked over to me.

"C'mon, Dillinger. They got her. Get baby girl out of here. Y'all don't need to see her like this," she told me.

"She better be alright or I'm snapping everybody in this bitch necks," I said in a menacing tone to let her know I wasn't playing.

I allowed Layla to escort us out of the room while we went to the family waiting room where Santos was sitting with Reign and Mateo. As soon as Reign saw me carrying the baby, she jumped out of her daddy's lap and ran right over to me.

"Can I see, Uncle Dilly?" she asked.

"Sure you can, baby." I smiled as Layla picked her up.

Reign peeked at Destiny before gasping. "Her pretty like me," she said.

That caused everyone to laugh. The innocence of a child was truly something special.

"Yes she is, baby girl." I smiled at her.

Reign went on to tell me all about her plans to play Barbies and everything else she could think of, with Destiny, and for the moment, I was able to take my mind off of what was going on in the room with Cherry.

I was beginning to be restless as I paced back and forth in the little waiting room. It felt as if it had been forever since they kicked us out of Cherry's hospital room, but yet nobody was telling us anything. The last time I asked for an update, they told me she was in surgery but never told me what for. My trigger finger was starting to twitch, and just when I felt as if I was ready to get on some John Q shit, the doctor came to talk to us.

"Mr. Rivera?" he inquired as he walked over to us.

"Yeah? Is she good? Can I see her?" I asked him.

"Ms. Adams is in fact going to be okay. She's resting right now. We're going to give it some time for the anesthesia to wear off. Ms. Adams suffered from what is called a uterine atony. Usually when a woman delivers a baby, the uterus contracts to stop the bleeding where the placenta once was. In her case, it didn't do that, which caused some very serious and heavy bleeding, also known as hemorrhaging. I couldn't get the bleeding to stop, so I had to perform a full hysterectomy and remove her uterus. It was successful, and the bleeding did in fact stop. Like I said, she's resting now, but you're free to go back to see her," he explained to me.

"Thank you, doc. I appreciate it," I let him know.

I was at peace knowing that Cherokee was going to be okay. The fact that she had to have a hysterectomy didn't even matter to me. I never was the type to want a football team of kids anyway, so I was fine that I at least got two kids out of her.

"You go ahead and see her. I'm going to go check on Destiny," Layla told me. "I'll be in there in a few," she said.

I just nodded my head as I went to go check on my future wife. Since Santos had left with the kids to get some food, I pulled out my phone to shoot him a text to let him know that Cherokee was okay.

When I made it to her room, I walked in to see her sleeping so peacefully. Today had been a very eventful day for her, and I knew she was tired as hell, so I didn't bother her. I just walked over to the bed and kissed her on her forehead. She stirred a little, but she didn't wake up.

I sat in the chair next to the bed watching her. I really had to get my shit together when it came to this woman. There was nothing in this world that I wouldn't do to spend the rest of my life with her. I was tired of all the back and forth between the two of us. I just wanted to be a happy family with just her and my kids.

"Yes," she said lowly.

If I wouldn't have been looking at her, I probably wouldn't have heard her.

"Yes, what?" I asked as I walked over closer to her.

"Ask me again so I can say yes," she said as she could barely open her eyes. "Only if you still want me to be your wife," she slurred.

I just stood there in astonishment. I couldn't believe what I was hearing as I looked down at her with a big ass smile.

"Cherokee, will you marry me?" I asked her.

"Mhmm. Now hurry up and put my ring on before I change my mind," she said.

Damn, the ring.

I hadn't planned on this happening, so I didn't have the ring on me. It was sitting at home on my nightstand, not being touched since the day she turned down my first proposal. I wouldn't front like I wasn't salty as hell about her saying no, but I respected her decision and took the time to see where she was coming from on the matter.

"Cherry, I don't have the ring on me, baby, but as soon as Layla comes in here, I can go home and get it.

"Don't bother, it's okay. My answer is still yes," she said softly.

I wanted to ask her what made her have a change of heart, but to be perfectly honest, it really didn't fucking matter to me.

"I love you," I said while kissing her lips.

"I love you too. Where's my babies? I want them," she said as she looked around for the kids.

"Destiny is in the nursery, Lay went to go check on her, and Tae is with Santos, but they should be on their way back," I told her.

"Tell them to bring me my baby. I want her in here with me," she said.

I obliged and pushed the call button for the nurse to let her know Cherokee wanted Destiny back in the room with her. I couldn't wait for her to get out of the hospital so we could start the planning process of our wedding. I honestly would be fine with us just going to the courthouse and skipping the idea of a big wedding. I had been through all that already before.

11

Jacier

$\mathcal{M}$y leg bounced up and down anxiously as I sat at the table with my arms folded over my chest. I honestly couldn't even believe that I was doing this shit, but my sister was right. It was time for me to forgive Danielle, even if the bitch was not sorry. This was for me, not for her. I decided to do this sit down with her in a public place so I would be less likely to want to snap her fucking neck with a whole bunch of people around. I told Nova I was going to try, but I wasn't making any fucking promises.

The door to the restaurant opened, and there she was. Even though I hated her ass right now, I couldn't deny how beautiful Danielle was. She had a smooth peanut butter complexion with a few scars here and there but nothing that took away from her beauty. Her eyes were big and round, and she had a cute button nose and a full set of lips. She stood tall like a stallion as if she should've been someone's model.

Looking at her, it wasn't hard to tell why a nigga had fallen so hard for her, but at the same time, I felt dumb as fuck for doing so knowing what I knew about her.

"Hi," she said as she sat at the table with her head down as if she was afraid to look at me.

"Waddup," was all I said.

There was an awkward silence between the two of us before she lifted her head up to say something just as I was talking.

"Oh, go ahead," she said quickly.

"Nah, *you* go ahead. I came into this willing to hear you out so just say whatever it is you feel you need to say so we can be done with this for good," I let her know.

She pushed her hair behind her ear, which was a giveaway sign that she was nervous. I watched her intently as she shifted in the chair, preparing to speak.

"Honestly, there's nothing that I can say to make this shit right. As I told you before, it was nothing like you thought it was," she said.

"How you figure? I saw the video of you and this nigga... Yeah, just know I seen the proof," I let her know.

"You may have, but like I said, it wasn't what you thought it was, Jacier."

"You keep saying that, but you not fucking elaborating on the shit. So exactly what the fuck was it then?" I shouted.

Danielle looked around the restaurant in embarrassment, but I didn't give a fuck. I was giving her an opportunity to tell me whatever it was she felt I needed to know about the night she fucked my so-called best friend, but she wasn't saying shit.

"I was set up, Jacier. Your best friend and my best friend conspired together to drug me to get some info out of me. What was supposed to be a girls' night ended up in me being drugged by them. Rich thought you were trying to axe him out of the equation or whatever the shit may have been; I honestly don't know. He figured I was going to run my mouth to Alana about the shit, but when that didn't work, they took the shit to a whole other level. All I remember was that nigga coming to see her, he made us drinks, then the next thing I know, I was waking up in the bed next to Alana, naked. I heard Rich on the phone in the bathroom yelling about a hit gone wrong because they shot the wrong person," Danielle explained.

Hearing that, I sat up in my seat at that revelation. I always felt like the bullets Nyomi were hit with were never meant for her. I had let her drive one of my cars that night she was killed because hers was in the shop. Deep down in my gut, I knew whoever shot her was gunning for me. The police wrote it off as a drive by, and her case was cold, but I knew better. If Danielle was saying what the fuck I think she was saying, then fuck letting bygones be bygones. That nigga was going to pay.

"What the fuck you mean a hit gone wrong?" I asked.

"Nyomi, Jacier. Rich is responsible for killing Nyomi," she said softly.

Even though my blood was fucking boiling right now, I had to remain calm until I got all the facts.

"If what the fuck you saying is true, why the fuck you didn't tell me this shit when it happened? Why wait until this nigga exposed you?" I asked.

"I didn't even know there was video footage from that night, Jacier. Plus, Rich made it very clear that if I said anything, he was going to slit my fucking throat and do the same to my mama. I wanted to tell you, but you were grieving, and you know how you get," she explained.

"Why the fuck should I believe you? How do I know you're not lying to me?" I inquired.

"I don't have shit to gain by lying to you, Jacier. Before this incident even took place, we never had any problems. I have to look at my son every day and try not to resent him because of who his daddy is. You thought I was being sheisty, but I honestly had no idea that he was Rich's son. Regardless of what you may think, it was only that one time, and it was not consensual."

Maybe I was being dumb again, but I believed her. Thinking back, Rich was starting to move a little funny, but I never thought anything of it. Then he started to distance himself after we lost Nyomi. When he showed me that video of him fucking Danielle when he found out she was pregnant, I damn near beat the fuck out of his ass. The only reason I let the nigga continue to breathe was because of the brotherly bond we once shared. Now that I knew that nigga played a part in Nyomi's death, he had to pay.

* * *

"YOU REALLY BELIEVE HER?" Nova asked as she stood in the doorway of the room I used whenever I came to visit her.

"Yeah, I do," I answered without hesitation.

After my sit down with Danielle, I had to go visit Nyomi. I smoked blunts back to back while I sat at her gravesite and just talked to her. I hadn't been to her grave since the day of her funeral, but I had to go see her today. Outside of Nova, she was the only one who knew me better than anyone. Everybody always swore we had something going on because of how close we were, but that was never the case. Our relationship had always been strictly platonic, and messing with her would've been the equivalent of messing with Nova in my eyes.

I sat there for hours just catching her up on how Nyami was doing, what I had been up to, my crazy ass situation with Layla, and the shit Danielle had hit me with. I cracked a few jokes and talked a little shit before I let her know how she had fucked me up by leaving me.

After visiting with her, I came home and told Nova everything Danielle told me.

"Jacier, you—"

"I don't want to hear it, Nova. Ain't no talking me out of this shit, because I already made up in my mind that this is what the fuck I'm going to do," I snapped without meaning to.

"I'm just going to fall back because you coming real out of body with me right now for no damn reason. I was only going to tell your stupid ass to make sure you came home to your daughter since you think you know every fucking thing," Nova snapped back.

I sighed as my sister stomped away from my room. I knew I had fucked up if she was talking to me like that. Nova was a very sweet individual and was all about speaking life into people, so I knew she was pissed off at me if she was talking to me like that. Before I could even go after her to apologize, my phone started ringing. A small smile crept across my face when I saw who it was.

"Princess Lay." I answered the call. "Waddup, beautiful?"

I had called her earlier, but she didn't answer, so I guess this was her returning my phone call.

"Hey, sorry I missed your call earlier. I was at the hospital visiting Cherokee," she said into the phone.

"Hospital? She okay?" I asked, truly concerned.

I had really taken a liking to Cherokee the little time I had spent around her. She had a genuine heart and let me know off bat that she wasn't going to play any games with me when it came to her best friend, and I couldn't do anything but respect it.

"Yeah. She had a little fall that caused her to go into labor. She had some complications, but she's good. Her and the baby are good," Layla told me.

"Damn, I'm gon' have to send her a little push gift or whatever y'all call them shits. What about you, though. How you doing, Princess Lay?" I inquired.

Together or not, the love I had for her hadn't faded. Regardless of what we went through, I always wanted to make sure she was straight. That was why I kept sending her little gifts and shit to let her know that I was thinking about her. I also wanted to let her know there was no bad blood on my end. I just had to step back and remove myself from the equation because I felt like we were on two different pages in two completely different books.

"I've been okay. I could complain, but I won't because it would be pointless," she said into the phone. "How have you been?" Layla asked.

"I ain't een gon' lie, shawty. I been real fucked up for more reasons than one," I told her honestly.

"Why? What's wrong?" she asked.

Before I could even answer, I heard a voice in the background that halted me from explaining exactly what I had been going through. I didn't even have to wonder who the voice belonged to because it was clear as day.

So she back with that nigga?

Of course she was. Why wouldn't she be? Just as I had assumed, Layla's heart was still with that nigga Santos, and I had been wasting my time trying to be the man I had thought she needed in her life. I didn't regret none of the time we spent together, but I definitely did learn my lesson to never be a chick's rebound.

I let out a small chuckle before speaking. "I see you a little preoccupied, so I'm gon let you go." My words had more than one meaning.

"Wait—"

Before she could even finish what she was saying, I hung up the phone. I had bigger fish to fry right now. Walking to the closet, I went to the back of it where I kept a safe. I punched in the code that granted me access. I reached in and gabbed two of my Glocks that I kept in there before stuffing them in the waistline of my pants.

I grabbed a black hoodie, throwing it over my head, making sure my weapons were concealed under it. Walking out of the room, I did my nightly routine of going to check on Nyami to make sure she was straight. When I got to her room, I noticed she wasn't in there, so I knew she was with her auntie.

As I made my way down the stairs, I could smell the sage Nova was burning. I guess that was her way of subtly letting me know that I was a bad vibe. I went to the living room where I found Nyami in her swing, sleeping peacefully. I kissed her chubby cheek before making my way over to Nova and doing the same.

"I love you and I'm sorry, okay?" I told her.

"I love you too," Nova said.

I placed a kiss on her forehead before making my way out the house. I jumped in my truck before speeding out of the driveway. I wish I could say that this was a joyride, but unfortunately, it wasn't. I was on my way to handle that nigga Rich for once and for all. It wouldn't be hard to find that nigga because he was one of those types that loved being in the hood.

We grew up in Zone 6, Lil Mexico to be exact, which was also known as Kirkwood. Don't get it twisted though; none of the niggas from there were Mexican. Niggas proudly rocked the American flag but were far from patriotic. I couldn't even tell you all the shit I had gotten into growing up out there. Niggas like Rich glorified living in poverty, having to rob, steal, and kill just to get by. They swore that shit was a badge of honor.

Don't get me wrong, by no means was I ashamed of where I came from, but you would never catch me kicking it out there all day, every day. Just because you loved yo' hood and where you came from didn't mean it loved you back. It would be yo' own people that would be the ones to take you out. I had seen the shit happen first hand on many occasions.

Just like I knew he would be, Rich had his dumb ass right in the middle of the hood. I parked where I wouldn't be noticed and killed my headlights. I watched him for a few, disgusted about how he could just kick it like this like he wasn't a fucking snake. How he could live with himself knowing that he was responsible for killing our best friend honestly had me baffled.

I didn't have time to dwell on what went wrong or why he turned on us like he did, because I honestly didn't give a fuck. I came here to take this nigga out his misery, and that was exactly what I planned to do. Reaching into my glove compartment, I grabbed my flag bandana, stuffing it into my back pocket before taking one of my guns and cocking it.

I jumped out of my truck, throwing my hood over my head as I made my way over to where Rich was posted up, talking shit to some little niggas. One of the little niggas noticed me before Rich did and pulled his gun. I kept it moving, not even the least bit fazed. Rich looked at me with squinted eyes, but I guess recognition set in as he told the little nigga to chill and lower his gun.

"Muthufuckin Trouble." Rich laughed like something was funny. "Fuck you doing 'round these parts? I'm surprised you remembered where the fuck it was at, big time," Rich taunted.

His demeanor just further let me know that Danielle hadn't been lying to me earlier. Everything about this nigga screamed snake ass nigga. I didn't know how I couldn't see the shit back then, but I was hipped to it now.

"Time to pay the piper, nigga," I said as I took my hood off and pulled my gun. I wanted this nigga to look me dead in my eyes before I put a bullet in his fucking head.

I didn't know if this nigga forgot exactly who the fuck I was or what I was capable of or what, by the way he laughed in my face. His laughter was cut short though by the bullet that left the chamber of my gun.

Pow!

I turned my gun to the little nigga who had his gun pointed at me earlier and pulled the trigger.

Pow!

I spat on Rich's body before swiftly walking back to my truck. I wasn't worried about anyone dropping the dime on my ass about these murders I had just committed. I was well known around these parts, and plus, the cops weren't too quick to solve any murders in the hood anyways.

That nigga I had worked so hard to bury was now back at the surface, and I didn't know if I would be able to get rid of him once again. Muthufuckas wanted Trouble back so bad, now they had him.

12

Layla

"*How* ow about this color, Lay Lay?" Reign asked as she picked up a pretty purple that she wanted her nails.

Every two weeks, I got my nails done like clockwork, and now I had Reign to accompany me. She was so precious and such a joy to be around that I could never see myself being mad at her or taking my anger out on her for her father's choices.

I had always wanted a mini me, and it seemed as if when Reign and I started getting close, that was exactly what I got. I couldn't wait for Destiny to get older so I could spoil both of my girls.

"That's pretty, baby. We can do that color," I told her just as my phone dinged with a text from her daddy.

Santos: *When ya'll coming back?*

Me: *We're just now picking out our color, Santos.*

Against my better judgement, I had taken Santos back, and we were slowly working on our relationship. It wasn't really like I had a choice any damn way. This man was so relentless and wouldn't let up. This nigga had basically bullied me into giving him another chance. This was it though. If he fucked up this time, I was done with Santos for good.

I looked up as the door chimed, signaling that someone had just walked in the nail shop. I saw two girls walk in, but I paid them no mind as I let my nail tech know that we had our color picked out.

"Girl, that nigga Santos fucked me so good the other day my pussy still throbbing," one of the bitches said.

I raised my brow as I glanced over at Reign, making sure she hadn't heard what the ghetto bitch had said, but she was very inquisitive and caught on to things easily.

"Lay Lay, why her say my daddy name?" she asked.

I raised up my phone, snapping a picture and sending it to Santos.

Me: *Who this bitch???*

"Girl, I didn't know you started back fucking him again."

"Again? Girl we never stopped. He had gotten into a little situation where he was out of commission for a while, but once he came back, he dived right into this pussy because he couldn't get enough and missed it. His words," the bitch with the bad weave said.

Santos: *Don't start this shit, Lay. I don't know them bitches.*

I couldn't do anything but laugh because I knew his ass was laying. The only reason I wasn't going to cut up in this bitch was because I had Reign with me. I was going to chill for now, but this nigga was definitely going to hear my mouth when I got back to his house.

It was shit like this that made me weary about taking this man back. There was no telling how many bitches he had stuck his dick in. Had this been five years ago, no bitch would've ever been bold enough to brag about how she was fucking and sucking Santos. A nigga that was supposed to be mine and mine only. This was some shit that I just couldn't get jiggy with.

I was snapped out of my thoughts by the incoming FaceTime call coming through on my phone. With a smile on my face, I answered as Nova's face popped up on my screen.

"Hey, beautiful? How are you?" she asked.

"I'm fine, gorgeous. How are you?" I threw back at her.

I loved me some damn Nova. No matter what her brother and I went through, she always made sure she kept in touch with me. She was so stinky cute and sweet that I took her on as my honorary little sister.

"I would be better if you came and got this pain in the ass I call a brother off my hands," she rolled her eyes.

I just chuckled while shaking my head. "Nova." I sighed.

"I know, I know, but I just have this gut feeling that you two are going to work it out. My gut has never lied to me. But anywho, that's not why I called you. I actually wanted to ask you something," she said.

"What's up? I'm all ears," I let her know.

"Well, my birthday is coming up in a month in a half, and I was just wondering if you could come to Atlanta to celebrate with me. You and Cherokee, if she can take a small break from mommy duties. If not, I completely understand," Nova said.

"Girl, what? You know I'm always down for a turn up. I been needing a getaway from this hellhole of a city anyway, so of course I'll come. I'm pretty sure Cherokee is down for the getdown too, but I can ask her to be sure," I let her know.

"Yay! I'm so excited, and I don't even get excited about my birthdays anymore. Let me know what she says, please ma'am."

I laughed at the fact that she called me ma'am like I wasn't only five years older than her. After assuring her that I would be sure to ask Cherokee, we ended our phone call. Instantly, my mind wandered to the idea of me seeing Jacier when I went to go celebrate his sister's birthday.

From what Nova told me, he still traveled back and forth from Miami to Atlanta, but I honestly hadn't seen him in a while. He had called me a while back, but I missed his call due to me being at the hospital, checking on Cherokee and the baby. I was excited to see that he called me that I wasted no time returning his phone call.

I obviously was too anxious to do so because I had momentarily forgot that Santos was at my house. That was until he came into my room, talking loud as hell. Of course Jacier heard him and hung up on me. To say that I was crushed would be an understatement. I had been missing Jacier like crazy, and the one time he reached out to me, backfired.

I had reached out to him numerous of times after that, but it was to no avail, because they all went unanswered without a response. I finally caught the hint and gave up, which ultimately led to my decision to take Santos back. I didn't want to say that Santos was a second option or anything, because that wasn't the case. It was just that I finally stopped the battle between my mind and my heart.

I HAD SUCCESSFULLY LEFT the nail shop without cutting a bitch. I kept my headphones in until we left just so I could tune the ghetto twins out. Reign informed me that she wanted some chicken nuggets, so after getting her something to eat, we were headed to her daddy's house. My phone started ringing, and I hit the Bluetooth to answer the phone for my brother.

"What's up, A'mir?" I answered.

"Lay Lay, come get me before I kill this bitch!" A'mir yelled into the phone.

His yelling was followed by a lot of commotion with somebody else yelling obscenities at him in the background. I didn't even have to ask him what the hell was going on because I already had pieced together what it was. His dumb ass had taken himself back over there to the crazy bitch he had been supposed to left alone.

A'mir had an on again, off again bitch he had been messing with since I was a teenager. The two had never been in a relationship, and I was guessing the sex kept them fucking around with each other longer than they should have. I couldn't tell you how many fights the two of them had gotten into over the years.

Ginger had stabbed my brother, attacked bitches she had seen him with, totaled every car he had ever owned, and was the reason behind his latest prison stint. My other brothers and I had told him too many times to leave the crazy bitch alone before she killed him, but I guess the bitch's pussy was made of gold because he wasn't hearing shit we had to say.

Hanging up on his dumb ass, I sighed irritably as I rerouted and made my way to this damn girl's house. He knew he had to call me because Amaad wouldn't go get him and Akil would beat his ass for even being there. No matter how much shit A'mir talked about me being a cry baby or coddled me, he knew his baby sister was coming through any time he needed me.

It took me a total of fifteen minutes to get to her house. Before I could even pull up, I could see the commotion that was taking place in her front yard. My brother's Ferrari was fucked up. Tires flat, windows busted out as well as the headlights and taillights. She had even carved 'stupid bitch' on the red exterior of the car.

When I pulled up, I saw Ginger chasing my brother around the yard with a metal bat. I shook my head at the spectacle these two were causing.

"Reign, baby, stay in the car and eat your chicken nuggets, and I'll be right back, okay?"

"Okay," she said.

Grabbing my baby nine out of my purse, I stuffed it in my pants before jumping out of the car.

"Get in the fucking car, A'mir," I said with my voice full of irritation.

"Stay the fuck out of this, A'Layla! I don't even know why you're here, because this don't have shit to do with you!" Ginger yelled.

"Bitch, don't tell me what the fuck to do when it comes to my fucking brother," I spat at her.

I yanked A'mir by his shirt like he was my damn child to drag him to my damn truck. I guess Ginger though that was leeway for her to come after my brother because she came charging at him with the bat. A'mir moved out of the way and put his arm up to shield her from hitting him in the head with the bat. Instead, it hit him in the arm with a loud crack.

As my brother yelled out in agony, I saw red. My brothers weren't the type to put their hands on women. If they were, Ginger's head would've been knocked off her fucking head. Me on the other hand, I wanted *all* the smoke behind my fucking brothers.

"Bitch, is you fucking crazy?" I yelled out as I removed the gun from my waistline.

Before she could even blink, I slapped her across the face with it. She cried out as I continuously brought my gun down on her face. I was giving this bitch the ass whooping I should've given her years ago.

"Lay Lay, Chill! A'Layla, chill the fuck out!" A'mir yelled. "Get yo' crazy ass in the car before yo' dumb ass go to jail!" he said.

Smacking my lips, I pushed him off of me as I made my way back to my car.

"If it wasn't for yo' stupid ass, I wouldn't even be over here. What the fuck is you doing over here anyway? You must want this bitch to kill you?" I yelled at my dumb ass brother.

"Excuse me, A'Layla, but I thought I was grown. I didn't know I had to answer to you or anybody else," A'mir said as I sped off.

"You're dumb as hell, A'mir. You're just not going to learn, huh? How many more times is this bitch going to hurt you before you realize you need to let it go?" I asked, truly confused.

"You need to be asking yourself that shit, A'Layla. How many more times is Santos going to hurt you before yo' dumb ass lets him go?" he spat.

I wasn't going to admit it out loud to his ass, but his words cut me like a jagged edge sword. I had asked myself that question plenty of times, but to hear it coming out of my brethren's mouth had done something to me. Even though A'mir was an asshole, he was the only one who gave shit to me straight with no chaser. He had no qualms about hurting my feelings when he felt I really needed it.

I glanced in the rearview mirror at Reign who thankfully had been too engrossed in her tablet to notice I was out there showing my ass. That was probably one of the main reasons why my ass didn't need kids right now. Sometimes, I didn't know how to act. If anyone would've saw me out there acting a damn fool, I honestly could lose my social work license.

I gotta get it the fuck together.

A'mir sighed before he rubbed his hands down his face. "My bad, Lay Lay. I ain't mean to say it like that. You needed to hear it, but I ain't have to say it like that," he clarified.

I didn't even bother to respond because I had nothing to say. I wasn't in the mood to have this conversation with him or anybody else for that matter. Just like he wanted to holler about how he was grown, I was too and didn't have to explain my choices and decisions to nobody.

Cherokee

J sat on the swing of the beach house with Destiny in my
arms as I watched Dillinger and Mateo run around on the
beach playing. I smiled at how drastically my life had changed in only
a month and a half. I was now a mother of two and a wife. Yes, you
read that right. I was officially Mrs. Dillinger Rivera. The day I got out
of the hospital, Dillinger and I had snuck off to the courthouse and
gotten married, per my idea.

I told him that I didn't need the big wedding shenanigans. If he was
serious about wanting to make me his wife, I was ready right then and
there. I knew I said I wasn't ready to marry Dillinger, but after I had

my daughter, I swear I had an epiphany. I realized I didn't want to be with nobody but Dillinger, as crazy as it seemed.

I ran out on him for eight years, but the moment we came back in contact with each other, we were inseparable. It was as if we picked up where we left off. As much as I tried to fight it, I loved this man with everything in me, and I didn't think I could ever love someone as much as I loved him. So it seemed as if it was only right that we put our bullshit to the side to become one.

"Your godmom is calling us, pretty girl," I said as I answered Layla's FaceTime.

"Bitch, where you at with my fucking daughter?" Layla asked.

"Why must you be so vulgar?" I laughed.

"Because you got me fucked up running off with my kids like that. You must not know that I will press charges on yo' ass for kidnapping," Layla told me.

"Get your panties out your ass, hoe. We're still in the city. Dillinger just brought us to his beach house for a day of family fun."

It was killing me not to tell Layla about our marriage for the simple fact that I told her everything, but I wanted to surprise her. Dillinger and I had a bet that I wouldn't be able to keep us being married a secret until after our honeymoon. Technically, this was our honeymoon since we didn't want to leave the kids.

"Okay, good. I was just confirming that you were still going to Atlanta with me for Nova's birthday," she said.

"Yes, girl, I'm going," I let her know.

"Umm, does Dillinger know?" she asked.

"Does Dillinger know what?" I heard, causing me to jump.

I was so caught up in my conversation with Layla that I hadn't even noticed that he and Mateo were no longer on the beach. He damn near scared the hell out of me, creeping up on me like that.

"Aw shit, I gotta go." Layla hung up.

"Does Dillinger know what?" he reiterated.

"That Nova asked Layla and I to come to Atlanta to celebrate her birthday with her," I told him.

"Who the fuck is Nova, and what the fuck makes you think you're going to Hotlanta to show yo' damn ass?" he asked.

I had to pause and catch myself from laughing at the look he had on his face. I knew he was being serious, but the look he was wearing was pretty comical.

"She's Jacier's sister, Dillinger. Besides, she's not even into the club scene, so it's going to be some good, clean, wholesome fun," I let him know.

"Cool. Let me text my nigga Santos and see if he's down for a lil' trip," he said as he pulled out his phone.

"What?" I screeched. "Dillinger, don't do that. That's so damn messy of you."

"How?" he asked with his face scrunched up.

"How?" I mocked him. "Why would you try to have Santos go knowing it's bad blood between him and Jacier—"

"So y'all *is* going to see that nigga, huh? Layla think she slick. Let me put my nigga up on game," Dillinger shook his head.

"No, stupid. Let me finish." I rolled my eyes.

"Continue," he said.

"Like I was saying, why would he go knowing that's Jacier's sister and it's bad blood between them? Besides, somebody has to stay here and watch the kids while we're gone, and that leaves you and Santos." I smiled as I got up to lay Destiny down.

I was trying not to make the same mistakes I did with Mateo and hold her all day to the point where you couldn't put her down without her crying, but I couldn't help it. She was so precious that I always wanted her in my arms.

"Hold the fuck up. So you think me and my boy some type of daddy daycare or something?" he asked.

"Yes." I laughed. "These are y'all kids just as much as they are ours. If we're being technical, Layla don't even have any kids. Being daddies for two day straight is not going to kill y'all." I rolled my eyes at him.

"I don't know about this shit, Cherry. I don't need no niggas thinking it's okay to push up on my fucking wife." Dillinger spat with his face contorted into a frown.

After laying Destiny down in the portable crib we brought with us, I turned to Dillinger as I led the way out of the room.

"Dilly, look. A nigga can have more money than you, be finer than you, with a dick bigger than yours, but that won't ever mean shit to me because all I want is you. All I see is you. You gave me your last name, and that was better than anything another nigga could give me," I told him.

"Wait, how you know it's niggas with a bigger dick than me?" he asked, causing me to laugh.

"Ugh, bye, Dillinger." I rolled my eyes at him.

Before I could walk away, Dillinger pulled me close to him, burying his face into my neck before kissing it lightly.

"Thank you," he said.

"For what?" I asked.

"For trusting me to be the man to make you happy for the rest of your life," he said before placing another kiss on my neck.

"No, thank you," I said.

"For?" he asked.

"For trusting me to carry and honor your last name, especially after the last time." I rolled my eyes.

"I don't know shit about a last time. You're my first and only wife," he told me.

I just shook my head, but I didn't bother to comment on it. If that's how he felt, then who was I to correct him?

14

Jacier

"*D*amn, girl," I said breathlessly as I released my kids into her mouth.

It was shit like this that I could get used to. I had been fucking with this lil' chick I ran into about a month back, and she was freaky as hell. I was talking about a real dick pleaser. I think that was one of the reasons we meshed so good; we both had a high ass sex drive.

After stuffing my now soft dick back into my pants, she sat up, wiping her mouth. I laid my head back on the headrest as I tried to catch my bearings. I looked over at her as she swished some mouthwash around in her mouth.

"You the only person I know that carry mouthwash around on 'em." I chuckled.

CHARMANIE SAQUEA

"Can't be meeting your sister with your dick still on my mouth." She smiled after opening the door to spit out the mouthwash.

I just smirked as I opened the car door to get out, but I didn't really bother to comment on what she had just said. I hadn't really invited her so she could meet my sister. In fact, I hadn't invited her ass at all. I just so happened to be casually telling her about my sister's plans for her birthday, and she said that she would love to come with me. Seeing that she was cool as hell, I didn't really see the problem.

This was a first and last time thing though. I didn't need her getting the idea that I was trying to settle down or anything like it. I tried my hand at that shit, and it didn't work out both times, so now I was just doing me.

When we walked into the building, Nova rushed over to me with her face scrunched up.

"You're late," she said with a vicious ass roll of her eyes. "Who the hell is this?" she asked when the girl walked up, wrapping her arm around my arm.

"This Ashley. Ashley, this my sister, Nova," I introduced.

"Hi, it's nice to finally meet you," Ashley gushed.

Nova just looked her up and down before sucking her teeth and walking off. I just shook my head, but I wasn't surprised by her reaction. This was why I didn't bother bringing anyone around Nova; she didn't know how to act. You knew how people said a sister would kick it with whatever bitch her brother brought around? That wasn't the case for Nova. In fact, out of the two females that I'd ever brought around her, Layla was the only one she actually took a liking to.

Layla?

It was as if I had literally sat there and thought her ass up. Imagine my surprise when I walked over to the bowling lane where Nova led us to, to find Cherokee and Layla sitting there laughing. Everything came to a halt when I walked over with Ashley still hanging on my arm.

"What's up, y'all?" I spoke.

"Hey." Cherokee was the only one who spoke.

"Cherokee, I heard you have a new baby girl. Congrats on the new blessing." I smiled.

78

"Thank you, Jacier," she beamed. "Next time you come to Miami, drop Nyami off to me so I can see her. I miss her little pretty self," she said.

"I can do that," I told her. "Princess Lay, you can't speak?" I asked.

I let my eyes roam over her as she got up to grab her bowling ball. It had been months since the last time I saw her, and I couldn't deny the fact that she was still fine as fuck. I couldn't help but to lick my lips at the way her ass was looking in the shorts she was wearing. I just wanted to reach out and grab a handful.

She just turned around to look at me with a slight smirk on her face, but she didn't bother to speak. I just laughed, but I didn't press the issue.

"Y'all plan on getting in on this game, or y'all just gonna stay intertwined like a pretzel?" Jacieon asked.

"Fuck it. Add me to this shit so I can crush y'all. I'm tired of y'all talking shit," I told them.

"Oh, we got a billy bad ass on our hands, huh?" Layla laughed as she rolled the ball, getting a strike.

I just sucked my teeth as I waved her off. I wasn't impressed by all this shit talking she was doing. Jacieon had them split into teams and bet on the game. His team consisted of him, Layla, and Cherokee, while I had Nova and Ashley. We bet fifteen G's that my team would have the most points at the end of the game. He talked so much shit, and he knew I wasn't going to turn down some free money, so I accepted his challenge.

"C'mon, Lay. All we need is a strike, and we walking out this bitch with five thousand each." Cherokee coached her friend.

The game had been neck and neck up until now. Ashley had just rolled a damn gutter ball, so now we were down a few points.

"I got you, baby." Layla winked as she grabbed her ball.

I sat there with my arms folded as she rolled the ball, and I'll be damned if she didn't get a strike. I wasn't pressed about the money because my pockets weren't going to miss it.

"You can just give my money to Nova. I'm not going to do my girl like that on her birthday," Layla told me.

"That's so sweet and noble of you, Layla. But nigga, you can run me my shit," Jacieon said.

I just sucked my teeth at him because he was such an asshole. I watched as Layla walked away, heading toward the bathrooms. I waited for a few before I got up, following her.

"Where you going?" Ashley asked.

I just kept going, ignoring her. She wasn't my bitch, so therefore, I wasn't going to explain myself to her nor did I have to answer to her. Just as I reached the bathroom, Layla was coming out.

"Jacier, you scared… What are you doing?" she asked as I shoved her back in the bathroom, locking the door behind me.

I didn't bother answering her question as I smashed my lips against hers. She let out a small moan as I slid my tongue into her mouth, and that was all the ammo I needed to keep going.

"We can't," she said barely above a whisper as I moved my mouth down to her neck.

I ignored her as I simultaneously bit and sucked on her spot while unbuttoning her shorts.

"Jacier," she moaned.

"Tell me to stop and I will," I told her as I inserted my finger into her pussy.

I was hoping like hell she didn't say stop. Just by the way her pussy was gripping my finger had me ready to bust a nut. Instead of telling me to stop, she let out a moan. I felt her tugging at my pants, and it caused my dick to jump. Once she had my dick free, she tried to kneel down, but I stopped her.

"Naw, shawty. I just wanna please you," I told her.

There was no way in hell I was going to let Layla suck my dick when Ashley had just done so before I walked in this bitch. I know I was probably wrong for this, but I needed her. I needed A'Layla. Once I had her thong and shorts down, I lifted her up, sitting her on my shoulders. I walked over to the wall of the bathroom as I dived in head first into her pussy.

"Oh God," Layla cried out as I feasted on her as if I were famished.

Layla's scent was intoxicating. Hell, everything about her was intoxicating.

"Jacierrrrr! I missed you. I swear to God I missed you." She panted.

"You missed me, or you missed the way I eat on this pretty ass pussy?" I asked, never missing a beat.

"Both!"

I just laughed. I couldn't even be mad because at least she was honest. Once I felt her legs go stiff before they started to shake, I made my tongue go faster on her clit. Almost instantly, her juices were flowing in my mouth, and I made sure to lick up every drop. Layla was crying out about how she couldn't take no more and she just wanted to feel me. I happily obliged her. My dick was hard as a muthafucka anyway; the shit felt like it was about to break.

"Uhnn."

Layla and I both let out moans as I slowly slid into her. I had to pause once I was all the way in out of fear that I was going to bust already. The way she was biting her lip was doing something to me.

"Damn, girl. This pussy is dangerous," I said as I commenced to fucking the shit out of her.

I wasn't trying to make love to her ass right now. I was mad as fuck at her and had a lot of pinned up frustration that I planned on taking out on her pussy. All I wanted to do was love her chocolate ass and show her that not every nigga was out to hurt her, but I guess that wasn't good enough for her. Her heart was somewhere else, and I had to take my L and move the fuck on.

I had successfully been doing so by cutting off all communication with her ass, but the moment I laid eyes on her tonight, every feeling I ever felt for her came rushing back full throttle.

"Jacier, yes, right there. Please, right there," Layla moaned in my ear, driving me fucking crazy.

"Right here?" I asked as I continuously hit her spot.

"Yesss, yessss," she cried out.

"Ah fuck," I cussed.

I felt my nut building up as I pounded into her unmercifully. Layla quivered against me as she creamed all over my dick. I tried to hold back for as long as I could, but her pussy was lethal as fuck.

"Damn girl." I panted as we both fought to catch our breaths.

I slowly pulled out of her as I reached for a paper towel to wipe her so my nut wouldn't be dripping down her leg. After cleaning up, we both straightened out our clothes before walking out of the bathroom together.

For the duration of the night, Layla and I never exchanged any more words. I was pretty sure our people knew exactly what had happened by the sly looks they gave us when we got back to them. I didn't regret the shit that took place. I wanted Layla, and I knew she wanted me too, but I wasn't going to continue to be kept on the back burner until she figured out if she really wanted to be done with Santos or not.

15

Santos

"What's wrong with you?" I asked Layla.

Ever since she got back from her little trip to Atlanta, she had been acting different. I didn't question her on it, but I knew she saw that fuck boy while she was there. She didn't have to tell me because it was all in her demeanor. We were on good terms before she left, but now, she was distant. She had an attitude with me for no reason, and we were back arguing about stupid shit.

"Huh? Nothing, why?" she asked.

"Because I been sitting over here talking to you, but it's like I'm having a whole ass conversation with myself," I told her.

"I'm sorry. I just got a lot on my mind," she said.

"Oh yeah? A lot meaning that nigga you snuck to go see?" I questioned.

"What?" she asked with her face scrunched up, looking at me like I was stupid.

"Don't play me for a fucking fool, A'Layla. I know that was your whole purpose of going to Atlanta, just so you could see that nigga. I'm not stupid," I let her know.

"Obviously, you are stupid, because I definitely did not go there for him. It was for his sister. I don't even know why I'm up here explaining myself to you any fucking way. Ain't you the same nigga that had bitches gossiping about ya dick game at the nail salon?"

I just sucked my teeth in annoyance at the fact that she was bringing this shit up again. I won't lie, one of the bitches in the picture was the little bitch I fucked that day Reign and I went out for ice cream. I didn't know what Layla was on, so I told her I didn't know the bitches.

"Here you go with this shit. Anything to take the heat off of you, huh?"

"Fuck you, Rahiem. You wanna try to come for me just because you the one who been out here slinging dick like it's going out of style. If you fucked one of them bitches, then say it! That's why I don't trust your stupid ass now. You don't know how to keep it real," Layla spewed at me.

"Fuck it! Yeah I fucked the bitch! I fucked her in the bathroom of an ice cream shop. I fucked a few more times after that, but I don't even know the bitch name, Layla. She don't mean shit to me. It was just some pussy. Let that shit go!" I yelled.

Layla stood there looking at me as if she was disgusted, but I didn't care. She wanted to know so bad, but now that she knew, she couldn't handle it. She shouldn't even be mad in the first place because the shit happened before we even got back together.

"You so damn trifling. What the hell is wrong with you?" she spat.

"Aye, you wanted the real, so now you got it." I shrugged.

"So why the fuck you couldn't tell me that shit when I asked you the first time, Rahiem?" she asked.

I just threw my hands up and walked away. There clearly was no winning in this, so I was done talking about it. It really was a damned if I do, damned if I don't situation.

As I was making my way to the kitchen, I saw Reign standing at the top of the stairs with sad eyes at the same time that my doorbell rang.

"What's wrong, baby girl?" I asked her.

"Why you and Lay Lay fighting?" she asked with a pout.

"We're just having a little disagreement, baby. Everything is going to be okay," I told her.

"A dis a what?" Reign asked with her face scrunched up in confusion.

I laughed as I picked her up, carrying her back down the stairs as I heard Dillinger asking where I was at.

"I'm right here," I said as I made my way back into the living room.

"Uncle Dilly!" Reign yelled in excitement.

You couldn't tell her ass shit when it came to this ugly ass dude. Even though I was slightly jealous, I couldn't wait for Destiny to get older because I was going to be the exact same way with her.

"To what do I owe the pleasure of this visit?" I asked.

"We have something we wanted to share with you," Cherokee said.

"What's wrong?" I asked.

She looked over at Dillinger, and he nodded his head as if he was telling her it was okay to tell us.

"We're married!" she gushed.

"Wait, bitch, what?" Layla asked. "Since when?"

"Almost two months ago," Dillinger said nonchalantly.

"Two months?" Layla and I asked simultaneously.

"Congrats, nigga," I told Dillinger as I pulled him in for a brotherly hug.

"Bitch, let's go so you can hear my mouth." Layla fussed at Cherokee as she pulled her away from us, with Destiny in her arms and Reign trailing behind them.

"Let's go smoke," I said as I playfully air boxed with Mateo before he headed to the game room downstairs.

Dillinger and I went out on the back patio where I fired up a blunt I had previously rolled. We were silent for a few as we sat in the patio chairs just passing the blunt back and forth.

"So how does it feel to be a married man again?" I asked.

He laughed as he inhaled on the blunt, choking on the smoke. "Shut the fuck up, nigga,"

"Nah, I'm just talking shit though. I'm happy for y'all muthu-fuckas. At least one of us will have a happy ending," I said.

Here Dillinger was on his second marriage, and I couldn't even get my relationship with Layla back on track.

"I thought you and Layla were doing good?" he asked as he passed me the blunt back.

"Nah, hell nah. I thought we was gon' be able to work out our problems and put the bullshit aside so we can be happy together, but the shit not going how I imagined," I told him.

"It takes time, Santos. The shit not gon' come to you just like that," Dillinger said as he snapped his finger.

"How much more time, though? I'm starting to get frustrated. If you say you willing to forgive me, then why the fuck you keep throwing the shit up in my face or making snide remarks about me hiding shit whenever you get mad at me? I damn near be ready to throw the towel in and say fuck it. I'm not going to keep feeling like I'm forcing that damn girl to be with me," I told my right-hand man.

"Nigga, you are forcing her to be with you." Dillinger laughed.

"Go to hell." I cut my eyes at him.

"Real shit though, Santos. If you really want something, you have to fight for it, no matter how hard it seems. The easiest thing to do in a relationship is to leave and give up."

Crazy how this nigga had been married twice; now all of a sudden, he was a love guru, trying to give me advice and shit.

"Yeah, well enough about me. I see life been treating you well," I said.

"I have no complaints, but I did have something I wanted to talk to you about," he said.

"I'm all ears."

"I want out. I'm leaving the game," Dillinger said.

I let out a whistle as I took the blunt he was passing me. I didn't respond immediately, because I had to let his words marinate for a second. Me and this nigga jumped head first into this shit together. We started off running errands for the local drug dealers, to being some nickel and dime niggas, to moving up on the totem pole to being where we are now. *Together.*

"How long you been feeling like this?" I asked.

"Honestly, the thought been dancing around in my head since Maino took the kids, but the moment I looked into my baby girls' eyes, I knew I had to give this shit up. You know like I know this shit only lead you to two places: behind bars or to the grave. We don't know any nigga that was really successful in this shit. I just wanna be able to be around to watch my kids grow," he explained to me.

I nodded my head in understanding because I understood where he was coming from. Me though, I was a greedy nigga, and I was going to milk the game for everything I could before I called it quits.

"I respect it, Dilly. You know that I'm behind you on whatever you wanna do."

"Good. That's all I need. I'm just going to do this one last drop before I hand everything over. I figured you wouldn't be ready yet, so I was prepared to hand everything over to you. Besides, we built this shit together, so it's only right," he said.

We gave each other some dap as we continued to talk out our plan. I was proud of my right-hand man. He was doing this shit right and was everything I aspired to be right now. Hopefully, Layla and I would be able to get our shit together real soon. I was trying to be on some settle down with the love of my life type shit too.

Dillinger

I sighed heavily as I sluggishly walked into the house. I had been working my ass off to tie up all the loose ends I could before I retired. I couldn't even lie to you; a nigga was tired as fuck. I always said that I wanted to be a millionaire before I retired, and I was almost at my goal. I had been in grind mode nonstop, working long hours, late nights, and early mornings.

When all this was said and done, I was going to owe Cherokee the world. I had barely been home lately which meant that she was home with the kids by herself all day but once had she ever complained. She knew and understood the sacrifices I went through to make sure her and my kids would forever be straight.

After securing the alarm, I went upstairs to check on the kids. Mateo wasn't in his room, so I made my way across the hall to Destiny's nursery. Of course, he was in there, curled up in the rocking chair by her crib. I just smiled at my kids before backing out of the room.

I could already tell the two of them were going to have an unbreakable bond despite their nine-year age difference. Mateo was going to go to the end of the world to make sure that he protected his sister at all cost. He already didn't play when it came to her.

I tiptoed into my bedroom, expecting Cherokee to be sleep, but instead, she wasn't in the bed, and I heard the shower running in the bathroom.

"What you still doing up?" I asked her as she came out of the bathroom.

"I couldn't sleep. I saw you pull up on the security system, so I got up to get your shower ready for you," she said as she walked over to me to help me undress.

"You didn't have to do that, bae," I told her before placing a kiss on her lips.

"I know but I wanted to," she said softly.

Cherokee gently removed my clothes. Once she had my shirt off, she stood on her tippy toes, kissing the new tattoo I had of her name on my chest. I had already gotten her lips tattooed on my neck years ago, but I wanted her name across my heart so she'd know there would never be another.

I took her hand, kissing the tattoo she had on her ring finger of the date we got married with the word *Mrs.* right above it.

"I love you," I told her.

"I know. I never doubted it," Cherokee said as she led me into the bathroom.

I put my hand under the water to test it, and of course, she had it at the right temperature. I dropped my boxers as I took my hair out of the bun it was in, letting it flow down my back.

"You mind if I join you?" I heard from behind me.

Just as I was turning around, Cherokee opened her robe to show me that she had absolutely nothing on under it. She dropped it, just standing there in all her naked glory, making my mouth water. She was just about two months postpartum, and her body was still bad as fuck. She had some light stretch marks on her hips, but I was a real nigga, so the shit didn't faze me.

"Hell nah," I answered as I stepped back so she could get in the shower with me.

I watched her like a hawk with my lip tucked in between my teeth as she moved through the spacious shower. After grabbing our rags and body wash, she came and stood back in front of me. I peered down at her with hooded eyes that were full of love.

"Damn. I would've had yo' ass knocked up right about now," I told her as I grabbed two hands full of her ass, pulling her closer into me so she could feel the effect she had on me.

She looked down as she shifted her weight from one leg to the other. I placed my finger under her chin, lifting her head up so she was looking at me.

"Why the long face?" I asked as she took my dick into her hands, gently stroking it.

"Does it bother you? That I can't have any more kids? Be honest with me," she said.

"Honestly, no, it doesn't. You gave me something no one on this earth could ever say they gave me, and that's them two beautiful kids in the other room. I love you regardless. That shit don't make me look at you no differently," I told her, meaning every word.

With a smile that was bright enough to brighten up the darkest sky, Cherokee slowly lowered herself until she was eye level with my dick. She replaced her soft hand with her mouth, swallowing my already hard dick whole.

"Gottt damn."

Her mouth was so damn wet and warm that I started singing the Itsy Bitsy Spider in my head to keep from busting all ready. I placed my hand on the back of her head, tangling my fingers in her hair as her head bobbed up and down on my dick. I had to use my free hand to grab onto the shower wall to stop myself from falling when she made my knees buckle.

"Oh, you so damn nasty," I moaned.

When I looked down, I found Cherokee playing with her pussy while she sucked my dick with no hands. That was it. I couldn't take no more.

"Fuckkkk!" I yelled out as I released my kids down her throat.

Her crazy ass thought it was okay to keep going, even though I had already bust my nut. I had to yank her off my dick just for her to stop sucking.

"Fuck is you trying to do to me, girl?" I asked as I tried to catch my breath.

"Take care of you, love you, make you happy, relieve some stress." She shrugged. "Nothing too major." She smiled as she soaped up my rag and began to wash my body.

I didn't even know if it was possible, but I was seeming to fall more and more in love with this woman every day. She may not have been perfect, but she was perfect for me.

"So how do you plan on breaking the news about your retirement to the streets?" Santos asked as we prepared for our shipment to come in.

"Shit, honestly, I don't even know. Cherry said she wanna throw a nigga a retirement party, and I'm thinking about letting her," I told him.

My wife had been very supportive in my decision to quit the game. I wasn't surprised by that though. For one, Cherry never really liked the idea of me being in the streets. I also wasn't surprised, because that's just how Cherry was. She was very fucking supportive of the people she loved.

I could've told her I wanted to run a hot dog stand, and she would be right by my side asking muthufuckas if they wanted ketchup or mustard. That's why I loved her ass like I did.

"I still can't believe you really about to leave the game." Santos shook his head.

I ran my hands down my face because I honestly couldn't believe it either. I used to be one of those niggas who swore they were never gonna leave the game. All the money, cars, clothes, and bitches, why would I? I realized now that wasn't shit but a young nigga's mindset. I was damn near thirty years old; it was time to let the shit go and walk away from it while I still could.

Pulling my phone from my pocket, I scrunched my face up at the number I didn't recognize. I wasn't going to answer it, but against my better judgement, I did.

"Who this?" I answered.

"Mr. Rivera? My name is Doctor Toller, and I have your son, Mateo Rivera, as well as your daughter, Destiny Rivera here. They were brought in for—"

"Which hospital?" I cut him off.

"University," he answered.

I didn't even bother to say anything else as I hung up the phone. I could get all the info I needed when I got to the hospital.

"What's wrong?" Santos asked.

"I don't know. Some doctor called me from the hospital to let me know he got my kids," I said.

"You go ahead. I'll handle this then I'll be there," he said.

"Good looking," I told him before leaving the warehouse.

When I got in my truck, I pulled out my phone to call Cherokee to see if she was okay, but her phone was going straight to voicemail. I just shrugged it off, figuring that I would talk to her when I got to the hospital.

Traffic laws didn't exist for me as I sped to the hospital to see what was up with my kids. When I walked through the doors, I went straight to the desk to let them know I was there for my kids. I didn't see Cherokee in the waiting room, so I knew she was back there with them already. When I walked into the room, Mateo was sitting on the bed with a gauze on his forehead while Destiny was being held by a nurse.

"Tae, what happened?" I asked.

"It was a loud pop then the car started spinning out of control. We ran into something and crashed the car, so they brought us here," he said.

"Where's your mama?" I asked as I took my daughter from the nurse.

Mateo looked at me like he wanted to say something, but he didn't want to say it in front of the nurse. She gave him a small smile before letting me know that she would let the doctor know that I was there.

"They took her," he said.

"Who is they?" I asked.

"I don't know. I played sleep and kept my eyes closed. They were saying something I couldn't understand. They weren't speaking English. Mom wasn't moving in the front seat. They pulled her door open and snatched her out the car. I started yelling for her when I saw them putting her in a black truck, but they sped off," my son explained.

"So how did you and your sister get here?"

"The ambulance."

Before I could say anything else, the doctor walked into the room. He informed me that both Mateo and Destiny were okay. Thankfully, Destiny was strapped into her car seat the proper way, so she didn't have a cut or scratch on her. Mateo had a gash on his head from hitting his head on the window, but other than that, he was going to be fine.

"Children services are here, and they would like to speak with you," the doctor informed me.

"About what? We don't have shit to talk about," I let him know. "Let's go, Tae," I told my son.

"Mr. Rivera, I think it would be in your best interest—"

"I said I'm not talking to them muthufuckas. Now unless you want me to dislocate yo' fucking jaw, I advise you to get the fuck up out my damn face so I can get my muthufuckin kids home."

Instantly, his skin lost its color, making him pale as fuck as he rushed out of my way. I wasn't about to play with these damn white people about my kids. Fuck was they calling the fucking children services people for anyway. It wasn't like Cherokee just up and left the kids on the side of the road on her own.

93

Just when I thought I was going to be able to leave the game in peace and enjoy the rest of my life as a family man, muthufuckas wanted to bring the beast out of me one last time. Everybody knew I didn't play when it comes to my family. I guess they didn't catch the hint when they kidnapped my son.

I was turning this muthufuckin city upside down until I got my fucking wife back. and that's a promise.

17

Layla

J paced back and forth as I tried to rack my brain to figure out who would want to do something to my best friend. Cherokee was sweet as hell and didn't have no enemies. Dillinger and Santos couldn't figure out who was behind her disappearance either, because let them tell it, they didn't have any beef in the streets either after they handled Maino.

Now everyone was gathered over here at my brother's house trying to put their heads together to come up with a solution to our new-found problem.

"Come with me real quick," Akil whispered in my ear.

With a raised brow, I followed him up the stairs to the main level of the house. Since we were now away from everyone else, I could pick his brain.

"What's wrong?" I asked.

"Somebody is here to see you," he said.

"To see me?" I asked in confusion.

He didn't bother to respond as we walked out the front door. I stood there frozen when I saw exactly who my visitor was. I looked over at my brother in confusion, but he just shrugged his shoulders before going back into the house, closing the door behind him. I slowly walked over to Jacier, who was leaning up against his car, looking sexy as hell with Nyami in his arms.

"Princess Lay." He beamed as he gave me a smile that not only wet my panties, but it blinded me as well.

It was just something about this sexy, chocolate, country ass man standing right before me. I hadn't seen or heard from him since Nova's birthday party, but I wouldn't lie and say he hadn't been on my mind.

"Hey, you. What are you doing here?" I asked as he pulled me in for a hug.

Just like butter, I melted in this man's arms. It was crazy to me how something so simple as his touch made me relax instantly, and for the moment, I forgot all about my problems.

"I was chatting it up with Akil on some business shit when he told me about what happened to Cherokee. Of course I had to come through and check on you; it was only right. How you holding up?" he asked as I took Nyami from him.

I sighed as I shrugged my shoulders. "I'm holding up as best I could be. I just feel like I'm not helping her by sitting around on my ass, but at the same time, I don't know what else to do," I explained to him.

The only clue we had to Cherokee's disappearance was the fact that the men who took her, didn't speak English, from what Mateo said. The only thing that did was confuse us even more. Hell, we lived in Miami. They could've been speaking Spanish, French, Arabic, any language.

"I feel you. I been in your shoes before, and it ain't a god feeling.

You just gotta stay strong and make sure everyone else around you remain the same way. Whenever they feel like they're falling apart, you gotta be the one to keep 'em together."

"Yeah, you're right. How you been though?" I asked.

"Missing you," he said with a straight face.

I just cleared my throat as I shifted underneath his gaze. "How's it going with you and ol' girl? What's her name again?" I asked in reference to the girl he was with at his sister's birthday celebration.

"It's going." He shrugged. "Just like it is with the other bitches I fuck from time to time," he said like it was nothing.

"Wow," was all I could say.

I didn't know why, but hearing Jacier admit to fucking other bitches really disturbed me. Of course I knew he was; he was too damn fine to be celibate. I just didn't want to actually hear him say it.

"So, is that what I was? One of your bitches you fucked from time to time?"

I don't even know why I asked that shit, but I did. Jacier cocked his head back and looked at me like I was stupid before he chose to speak.

"Come the fuck on, shawty. Don't een insult me like that. You know exactly what the fuck it was witchu. I was all for you, and you was conflicted, so I fell the fuck back. I'm single now, so I do single nigga shit. Completely different situations," he said.

I had to fight back a smile while he was talking. It was so cute to me how thick his accent got when he was mad. Even with a deep scowl on his face, this man was sexy as hell. I didn't know why, but for some reason, my hand gravitated toward his face. I cuffed his face with my hand, and his face softened at my touch.

Next thing I knew, Jacier leaned down, pressing his soft lips against mine. The crazy thing was, I didn't even try to stop him. Not even when his slid his tongue into my mouth. I knew this was wrong, but how could it be when it felt too much like right? Jacier pulled away and stepped back away from me before reaching out for Nyami.

"We gon' get up outta here," he said as he turned to leave.

"Oh, okay," I said just above a whisper.

He didn't even spare me a second glance as he strapped Nyami into her car seat before he jumped in the car and sped off. I stood there confused about what caused the sudden shift in him, but I wasn't going to stress. I had other things to stress about like getting my best friend back home safely.

Sighing heavily, I walked back into the house where I found Akil standing in front of the window, watching us. I put my head down in shame as I tried to go back downstairs where everyone else was.

"Come here," he said, stopping in my tracks.

"What, Boopy?" I asked.

"Don't what me. Bring yo' ass here," he said.

I knew better than to try my brother, so I did as he said and went to see what he wanted.

"What you gon' do, Lay?" he asked when I reached him.

"Do about what?" I asked.

"You know exactly what I'm talking about. You can't keep playing this back and forth game. You saw firsthand just how ugly this shit can get. Now, I'm not saying you're responsible for either one of them being shot, because they are some grown ass man who are responsible for their own actions, but you gon' have to choose," he told me.

"Why can't I just have them both?" I whined. "Men be in polygamist relationships all the time, so why can't I do it?" I asked.

Akil just looked at me before he let out a small chortle. "The thing that disturbs me the most is that you're serious as fuck right now." He shook his head.

"Yes, I am. If you can't pick one, why not have them both?" I shrugged.

"A'Layla, listen to me. You are making this way more harder than it needs to be. Just follow your heart; it won't steer you wrong. Who is the first person you have on your mind when you wake up? Who is the one that crosses your mind in the middle of the day when you're busy? Whose name makes your heart flutter when you hear it? That's the person you choose to be with. I think deep down in your heart you already know who it is, but you're just afraid of the outcome," Akil told me.

I didn't say anything, because he was right. I knew exactly who I wanted to be with, but I was scared. I didn't know if I could handle being hurt anymore. I may just end up on an episode of *Snapped* if a nigga thought he was about to play with me again.

"Bullshit comes with any nigga that you're going to deal with. You just have to find one that's worth it because no relationship is perfect. I'm done giving out free advice after this. I'm about to start charging y'all muthufuckas for these good jewels I be dropping," my brother said before walking away.

I just shook my head at him before following him back downstairs to join everyone else. When we got down there, Santos walked over to me, looking concerned.

"You good?" he asked.

"Yeah... yeah, I'm good," I let him know as he pulled me into his arms.

I wrapped my arms around him, holding him tightly as if I were afraid to let him go. I just laid my head on his chest, enjoying the feel of his arms.

"I love you," he said as he kissed the top of my head.

I looked up at him, deep into his eyes. "I love you too," I let him know.

Cherokee

J paced the floor of the spacious bedroom, wondering how the fuck I even got here. More so, I was wondering what the fuck my capture wanted with me. I walked over to the window, peering out of it at the spacious lawn. I tried to open it, but of course it was sealed. There were some landscapers out there cutting bushes and working on the lawn, so I tried to bang on the window to get their attention. That was too no avail though; the window had to be about three stories up.

I heard the sounds of the door opening, so I quickly turned to see an older woman in a blue dress with a white apron on. It was the same woman who had been bringing me food for the past three days. She looked at the untouched tray of food before shaking her head and saying something in Spanish. She grabbed the tray and looked up at me.

"You no eat?" she asked.

"Help me," was all I said as I made my way over to her.

She looked at me with wild eyes before backing up. "No, no, no!" she said frantically before rushing out of the room.

Just before I reached the door, it was slammed shut. I twisted the knob, but just like all the other times I had tried it, it didn't budge, letting me know it locked from the outside. I screamed in frustration as I banged on the door.

"Get me the fuck out of here! I need to get home to my babies!" I yelled.

I hadn't seen my kids since the day my ass was snatched up. I didn't know if they were hurt or if they were okay. I had been locked up in this room with no communication with anyone except the little old lady who always brought me food. I swear I was starting to lose my mind in here. All I needed to know was that my kids were okay. That would give me some type of peace of mind.

I heard the doorknob jiggling, so I jumped up. The door came open, and in walked a man. He looked to be about six feet tall with a beautiful pecan skin complexion. He had beautiful wavy hair that was pulled back into a ponytail that hung down his back. His goatee was salt and pepper and was trimmed real neat as if he had just left the barber or something. His eyes were a mesmerizing honey color. His hands were stuffed in the pockets of his white linen short set that was accompanied by white loafers. The shirt to his suit was slightly unbuttoned at the top, showing off a chest that proved he worked out.

"Esmeralda told me you refuse to eat. Why is that?"

"Do you really think I'm going to sit up here and let you poison me?" I asked, dumbfounded.

He just slowly nodded his head as he turned to walk out of the room. He stopped in the doorway, slightly looking over his shoulder.

"Let's go," he said before he continued walking.

I stood there confused for a second, but I was happy to be finally leaving the confines of this damn room, so I obliged him. I stopped dead in my tracks when I saw the two burly men standing on both sides of the door with guns that were bigger than me.

"C'mon, mija. They're harmless until I tell them not to be," he said, never looking behind him.

"Who are you?" I asked.

He ignored me as he led me down the stairs. I damn near got dizzy coming down the spiral staircase and damn near tripped when I got to the bottom. Still not saying a word, he led me to the dining area where there was a big ass table. He walked over to a chair, pulling it out and gesturing for me to have a seat.

I slowly walked over to the chair, sitting down. I glanced out the window where I saw another man that was dressed the same as the other two upstairs, walking around the house with his gun laying on his shoulder.

Who the hell is this man?

Once again, I was wondering exactly where I was and who I was with. It was obvious by the house and the security detail that he was very wealthy as well as a very important man. He sat directly across the table from me at the other end. One arm was on the table in front of him, and the other arm was planted on the table by his elbow with his face resting on its palm.

"Excuse me, mija. It's just you're more beautiful in person."

"You don't know me," I told him as I looked at him through squinted eyes.

"I know more than you think I do," he said just as the same older woman from before walked in.

She had a big cart full of food that she was pushing around. He said something to her in Spanish, and she nodded her head before filling up his plate with food first before she made her way over to me. While she was placing the food on my plate, he dug into his food.

After she was gone, he looked up at me with an inquisitive look. "Go ahead. Eat your poison." He smiled.

I really didn't want to, but the more I inhaled the scent of the food in front of me, the more hunger pains I was hit with. Finally saying fuck it, I picked up the fork and dove in.

"So, you're not going to tell me who you are?" I asked after savoring the food I just put in my mouth.

I bullshit you not, it was seasoned to perfection. I definitely could tell that this wasn't American food I was eating, but it was good as hell.

"My name is Diego... Diego Rivera," he said smoothly.

It took me a minute for his words to hit me, and when they did, they hit me hard. I dropped the fork from my fingers, making it clink against the plate. My mouth fell open in shock as I looked at him.

"You're..."

"Yes, I am," was all he said.

He continued to eat while I sat there stuck. I had never met anyone in Dillinger's family, not even his mother. All I knew about her was that she was a drug addict and passed away from AIDS. He never spoke of his father, and after he blew up on me the first time for asking, I knew better than to ever bring him up again.

"Eat your food before it gets cold," he told me.

"What do you want from me?" I asked.

"Eat your food," he said as he looked up. "We can talk later."

I slowly nodded my head as I continued eating. For the duration of the time, we sat quietly. I was stuck in my own thoughts wondering how the hell this man knew who I was and exactly what he wanted with me.

After we were done eating, he led me to the den. He poured himself a drink and offered me one, but I respectfully declined.

"Where do you want me to start?" he asked.

"The beginning would be nice," I told him. "But we can just jump ahead to the part where you left your son fatherless."

He turned from looking out the window to look at me. It wasn't a hard or dangerous look. It was more so like his eyes were full of regret. He slowly sipped his drink before placing it on the table.

"Christina was a forbidden woman. Back then, it was frowned upon for a Cuban man to be involved with a black woman—"

"Wait, I thought Dillinger said he was Puerto Rican?" I cut him off.
He shook his head. "No, mija, I'm Cuban," he corrected me.

"Oh," was all I said.

"I met her one day while I was out handling business with my
brothers. She was with a group of friends, but she stuck out the most to
me. I slid her my number on the sly, without my brother's knowledge. I
honestly didn't think she would call me, but she did. From the first
conversation we had, I was smitten. She wasn't like other girls I had
ran across. Girls only wanted me because of my status and who I was.
Everyone knew who Estevan Rivera and his three sons were. They
knew one of us were being groomed to take over our father's throne as
the head of the cartel. Christina didn't give a damn about who I was.
She wanted me for me," he said as he looked up at me to make sure I
was following him.

I nodded my head to let him know I understood. It was the same for
me and Dillinger. His status in the streets didn't mean shit to me. I
loved him for him.

"As I said, it was frowned upon to mix races back then, so I had to
sneak around with her. I would have to pay my security detail not to
tell my father what I had going on." He laughed. "Imagine that, Diego
Rivera, the one who had been killing people since he was five, was
afraid to tell his father that he had fallen in love with a black woman."
He shook his head.

He took another sip of his drink before continuing on with his
story.

"Then, Christina found out she was pregnant. And that's when all
hell broke loose. To this day, I don't even know how he found out. I
had come in from going to Christina's very first doctor's appointment
with her when he beckoned me to his study. He asked me about it, and
I was honest with him. When I tell you that man beat my ass, he beat
the fuck out of me until my face was damn near unrecognizable. I
honestly think the only thing that kept him from killing me was my
mother's cries. After the beating, he shipped me back off to Cuba. I
had lost all contact with Christina. Years later, my father summoned
me back to the states. He had made the decision to choose me to be the

next head of the cartel, but there was only one stipulation," he explained.

"Dillinger," I answered.

He nodded his head. "I was not to reach out to Christina or have any contact with her or my child. I was torn, I really was, but I agreed to his terms. I didn't even know that the baby she was carrying was a boy until fate brought us back together one day. I've been in contact with Dillinger over the years, but not as his father, as his connect," he informed me.

"You never told him?" I asked.

"No, mija. I didn't know how. That's why I brought you here," he said.

I contorted my face into a frown at that revelation. "So you had me kidnapped to tell your son that you're not just his connect but also his father?" I asked for clarification.

He quickly shook his head. "That's not how I ordered things to be done, and trust me, those men were dealt with for handling you and the kids the way they did," he said as he gave me a look.

A shiver went down my spine at the way he said it. It was so crazy to me how much Dillinger looked like him in that split second. I was starting to see where he got his craziness from.

"He loves you, he trusts you more than anything in this world, he values your opinion. He doesn't make any decisions without considering you or his children," he informed me.

"How—"

"Don't ask, mija. Just know I know more than you would like to give me credit for." He cut me off.

"Okay. What do you want from me exactly?" I asked, still confused.

"He told me that he wants to retire from the game. It's funny because I myself plan on stepping down, but I have no one to leave my empire to. No one except my only child," he said.

I sighed heavily while grabbing my head. This was all starting to be a little too much for me. I think I actually would have rather this be one of those hostage scenarios where he wanted money from Dillinger for my return. At least I would've known what to expect. This though? This seemed way out of my control.

"So you want me to convince my husband to stay in the drug game? I don't know how much pull you think I have to talk him into doing something like that. What even makes you think I would be comfortable with him doing that?" I asked.

"What I do is different. It's not the normal hustle and bustle of the drug game. All I do is sit back and collect money from everyone who works for me. Nobody even has to see my face if I don't want them to. I have people who does the shipments for me, and whenever my people want to reup, they have a specific number to reach me at. I'm at the top of the totem pole," he explained to me.

I stood there stuck. This man, who I had never met before, was asking a lot of me right now. More than I was even sure I could give him. My only concern was that Dillinger would kill him before I could even explain what the hell was going on.

"Can you give me a minute to think about it?" I asked.

He nodded his head, assuring me that he would give me however much time I needed to think on it.

This shit is crazy as hell.

Santos

I threw the drink in front of me back as my mind raced. It was so much going on that the shit was starting to drive me crazy.

"You sure you wanna do this?" Akil asked me.

"Fuck no, but I don't have a choice. Her happiness means more than anything to me," I let him know.

I was really on some sap ass shit right now. I was about to do something that was going to cause me to lose my gangster card, but to be honest, I didn't even care.

"He on his way up," Akil said as he looked at the monitor behind me.

I enlisted his help so he could be a mediator of the sort to make sure things went down the way they were supposed to today. I had in my head how I wanted this meeting to go, but that didn't mean I wouldn't accidently let my temper get the best of me.

"Waddup," Jacier spoke as he walked into Akil's office.

Yes. I was putting my pride to the side and doing what I thought was the right thing. I wasn't no dummy. I knew Layla may have loved a nigga, but I also could see that she was no longer *in* love with me. Her touch didn't feel the same, her kiss didn't hold the same passion, her smile wasn't as bright as it used to be. At least not with me. I was dimming her light, and that wasn't something I ever wanted to do.

"I'm just gon' let y'all go ahead and do all the talking. I'm just here to make sure don't nobody walk outta here with bullet holes in 'em and shit," Akil explained.

As he was explaining what was going on, I was pouring myself another drink. I needed all the liquid courage I could get to help me do this.

"Shit, I know we've had our little problems in the past but—"

"Is that what you call trying to kill me? A little problem?" he asked with a raised brow.

"Yeah, a little problem," I told him. "Like I was saying, I'm past that shit. I'm throwing in the towel and bowing out gracefully. I fucked up and allowed another nigga to come in and make my girl happy. I was so sure that my spot in her life was solidified that I slipped up. In a major way. I'm a grown ass man who's learning, so I'm going to be a man and apologize for how I came at you and for trying to take you out the game. Had I never even fucked up, there wouldn't have been room for you to come in," I said.

The words tasted like bile as they left my mouth. I really couldn't believe that I was sitting here doing this right now.

"I can respect it. I also want to apologize on behalf of my peoples. They can be hardheaded as fuck sometimes. They went against me when I told them to leave it alone and also tried to kill you," he said.

I had already knew his people were responsible for trying to kill me if he wasn't the one who pulled the trigger himself. It was done and over with now, so there was no point in me even seeking retaliation. It would be pointless.

"Understood," I said.

"So help me comprehend exactly what you are telling me right now," he said.

"I'm telling you to learn from my mistake. Do right by Layla and make sure you keep that smile on her face so we won't have any more problems. I'm not promising to leave her life for good because, aside from being my girl, she was one of my best friends. That's the reason why I'm even putting her happiness before mine. Plus, my daughter loves her, so yeah. I'm saying, be the nigga I *thought* I was for her."

He nodded his head in understanding. "I'm gon' tell you just like I told her, I would never try to axe you completely out of her life. I understand the bond y'all had or whatever. Just as long as you and I have an understanding of the boundaries and shit, then I have no problem with y'all remaining friends. That's just the type of nigga I am."

"We got an understanding. I'm definitely going to fall back and let y'all be happy. Like I said, do right by her, nigga," I said as I stood up and extended my hand for him to shake.

He stood up, placing his hand in mine, and we gave each other a firm handshake. I wouldn't even lie like this shit was easy for me to do, because it wasn't, but I refused to have Layla miserable because she felt like I was forcing her to be with me. I loved her too much to have her resent me. If the only way I could have her in my life was as a friend, then so be it.

"That was very noble of you, nigga," Akil told me after Jacier left his office.

I didn't say anything as I finished off my drink.

* * *

I STOOD on the back patio as I watched Reign run wild in the backyard with laughter while Layla chased her. My heart smiled watching the two of them. This right here was a blatant reminder of why I didn't deserve Layla. I hid my daughter from her for two years. The daughter that I created when I stepped outside of our relationship.

Yet, she loved that little girl like she was her own. She held no hate or malice toward my daughter, and that was very commendable in my book. I damn near fell out when I saw how close the two of them were when I woke up from my coma. Layla didn't have to form a bond with Reign, but she did, even without me having to ask her to.

"Daddy!" Reign yelled when she noticed me.

I smiled widely as she ran over to me. I swooped her up in my arms while kissing her all over her face.

"Hey, you. How long you been here?" Layla asked when she made it over to us.

"Not too long," I told her. "I just got in from a little meeting," I told her.

"Was it a successful one?" she asked.

I nodded my head in the affirmative. "It was. Jacier and I came to an agreement," I let her know.

Layla froze before she slowly turned to look at me with her mouth agape.

"Reign, why don't you go find a movie for us to watch," I told her.

"Okay, Daddy!" she said before she took off running into the house.

"Why you… you—"

"Because I want you to be happy, and I'm not doing that for you," I told her honestly.

"Rahiem." She sighed.

She looked as if she was trying to find the right words to say. I could tell that she didn't want to admit to not being happy because she didn't want to hurt me.

"It's cool, Lay. I'm not mad nor am I hurt. If he makes you happy, why not be with him. I had my chance, and I fucked it up. I'm man enough to take my L and live with it. I still want us to remain close because, not only do I love you, Reign loves you too. You can't tell her shit when it comes to her Lay Lay." I smiled.

Layla laughed because she knew it was true. She had imprinted her love and charm on my daughter, so I wouldn't be able to get rid of her for good, even if I wanted to.

"Thank you," she said as she walked over to me.

She wrapped her arms around me and placed her heavy ass head on my chest. I kissed the top of her head before she stood on her tippy toes, placing a soft kiss on the corner of my mouth.

"You know I'll always love you, right?" I asked.

"I know. I'll always love you too," she said.

"Aye, make sure he treats you right, Lay, on some real shit," I told her.

"I will," she assured me.

Even though we may not have been in a relationship anymore, I was at peace knowing that our friendship would remain. It wasn't to get twisted though; I would always be one phone call away whenever Layla needed me. That shit would never change.

Dillinger

I pulled up to the compound that housed the address I was summoned to. I had only met with my connect a few times over the years, but it was never at this location. I pulled up to the gate and pushed the button.

"Si?" somebody answered.

"Uhh, I'm Dillinger. I came—"

"Ahh, yes, Dillinger, come in. He's waiting on you."

As soon as she said that, the gate opened, and I was granted access. I could just imagine how much money this muthafucka had to be living like this. I didn't know how many acres he was sitting on, but I knew it was a lot. This shit looked like a damn plantation.

I pulled into the circular driveway and jumped out of the car. I was met halfway my who I assumed was one of his henchmen.

He patted me down, and I was pretty sure he felt the two guns I had on me, but he didn't bother to confiscate them. He just nodded his head as he led me inside the big ass house. When I got in, I looked around like a kid inside a museum. This shit was laid the fuck out. I could only aspire to make enough money to be able to live like this. This was the type of shit I wanted my wife and kids in.

The henchman led me to a door before stopping and knocking. The voice on the other side said something in Spanish before the door opened.

"Dillinger, thank you for coming on such short notice," he said, getting up to shake my hand.

"No problem, Diego. I mean, did I really have a choice?" I asked.

He chortled a little before sitting back behind his desk. "You always have a choice, mijo."

"That may be true, but I heard the urgency in your voice, so I came when I was called," I let him know. "Exactly what did you want to talk to me about?" I asked.

Whatever he wanted was keeping me from finding my wife, but I wouldn't act as if I wasn't intrigued to know what he wanted to talk to me about. I honestly hadn't spoken to him since I informed him that I would be leaving the game.

"Hold on," he said as he pushed a button on his desk before speaking. "Come in, mija," he said.

I sat there in confusion as to what the hell was going on. I was starting to wonder if this shit was a setup, right before the door opened and I got the shock of my life. Instantly, my blood started to boil when I saw Cherokee walk in.

"Dillinger, no!" she yelled when I pulled my pistol and aimed it at Diego.

By me doing so, that caused his henchmen to draw their guns on me. It was two of them and only one of me, but I didn't give a damn. Cherokee rushed over to Diego and stood in front of my gun. I looked at her in confusion through squinted eyes.

"Somebody better tell me what the fuck going on before I go the fuck off in this bitch!" I spat.

"If you put the gun down, you could get all the explanation you need," Cherokee said.

"Lower your weapons," Diego ordered his men. "I said, now!" His voice boomed when they didn't follow his order the first time.

They may have lowered their guns, but I had yet to lower mine. Cherokee gave me a look that told me to stop playing with her, so I sucked my teeth before lowering my gun.

She walked over to me with her hand out.

"What I asked?"

"I don't trust your temper," she said.

"I'm not giving you my gun," I told her, shaking my head.

"Dillinger."

I groaned as I allowed her to seize both of my weapons. She sat in the chair next to me in front of Diego's desk.

"Thank you, mija," he said.

"Don't thank me just yet. You need to tell him." She sighed.

"Tell me what?" I was starting to get pissed off.

"I am your father," he said.

"What?" I exclaimed.

The only thing I knew about my dad was he wasn't shit. From my understanding, he ran off on my mom when he found out she was pregnant, leaving her to raise me all on my own. She was the only family I had outside of the one I created on my own. There was no way in hell this man was sitting here telling me that he was in fact my father.

"Tell him exactly what you told me," Cherokee said.

I looked at her with a perplexed grimace on my face. Diego sighed deeply before he went on to give me his spiel about how he was my father. I listened intently, hanging on to every word he was saying. I let him speak without interruptions because I wanted some understanding of this whole situation.

When he was done explaining himself, I sat there in my seat in astonishment, basically feeling everything I knew about this man was a lie.

"Damn," was all I could say. "Why would she lie like that?" I asked more so to myself.

"It was probably out of anger, rightfully so." Diego answered my rhetorical question.

I just looked up at him, not knowing what to say or knowing how to feel. Even though I was happy to know the nigga wasn't in fact a deadbeat in the historical sense of the word, I still missed out on having a father my whole life.

"So you knew who I was when Santos and I came to you?" I asked for clarification.

"No. I didn't put it together until a little later when I did some looking into the both of you. That was one of the main reasons I agreed to do business with you two. Aside from knowing you wouldn't bring me any heat or problems, I knew you were solid because you had my blood flowing through your veins. I didn't know how you would perceive me, so I didn't bother to tell you," he said.

I ran my hands down my face as I sat up to get a real good look at him. I could see some similarities, but I looked like my mama.

"I have any siblings?" I asked.

He solemnly shook his head. "No, it's just you. That's another thing I wanted to talk to you about," Diego said.

"Oh, so there's more?" I asked.

"I plan on retiring from being the connect, but I want the family business to stay in the family. I easily could give it to one of my nephews, but I feel that it's rightfully yours. My father passed it on to me, and I want to pass it on to my son," he explained.

I let out a whistle as the realization of what he was telling me hit me.

"How would your father feel about your mixed breed son taking over the family business?" I asked.

He shrugged his shoulders as if to say he didn't really give a fuck. "You're a Rivera. Like I said, it's rightfully yours."

Don't get me wrong, if I accepted this offer, I would be touching more money than I ever had in my whole life. But my decisions no longer affected just me. I had two kids and a wife I had to be considerate of. I glanced over at Cherry, and she just shrugged.

"I'm behind you with whatever you choose to do," she said.

I glanced back over at Diego, and I could see the anticipation dancing around in his eyes. This was a lot for me to take in right now. Just a few weeks ago, I was ready to be done with this shit, but now I was presented with a grand opportunity that would not only change my life, but everyone around me lives as well.

"I… I accept," I said.

I couldn't believe the words had come out of my mouth so effortlessly, but it was what it was. Diego sighed as if he was holding his breath. He himself probably couldn't believe I accepted his offer, but I would be one dumb ass nigga if I didn't. Besides, he said it himself; I'm a Rivera, so why not?

21

Layla

*J*laid on Jacier's chest, drawing imaginary circles as I listened to his heart beat. I honestly didn't think we would be back here again, but I was delighted that we were. I knew it took a lot out of Santos to let me go, but he knew like I did that it was for the better. It wasn't like I was in absolute misery with Santos, but I was no longer happy with him.

"What time is it?" Jacier asked drowsily.

"A little after nine in the morning," I answered.

"C'mon, get up. We got an appointment at eleven," he said as he slapped me on the ass.

"Appointment where?" I asked.

"You'll see when we get there," he told me as he sat up once I got off his chest.

"Okay." I shrugged as I climbed out of the bed.

"Aye, he said as he grabbed my hand. "You know I told you that I got you no matter what, right?" he asked.

"Yes," I answered without hesitation.

He kissed my lips before slapping me on my bare ass once again. "Start the shower. I'll be in there in a minute," he said.

Doing as he said, I went to the bathroom and started the shower, waiting for Jacier to join me. As soon as my body came in contact with the hot water, it immediately began to relax. I closed my eyes to enjoy the feel of the water against my skin, when I felt the cold draft, letting me know that my honey had finally decided to join me.

I let out a small giggle as he got behind me, burying his face in the crook of my neck. I turned around, standing up on my tippy toes to kiss his soft lips. I reached for his dick, but he grabbed my hand.

"C'mon, shawty. I told you we had somewhere to be, and you know how you get," he said.

"I just wanted to have a little fun." I pouted.

He looked down at me through hooded eyes before taking his lip into his mouth.

"Put yo' leg up," he said.

Feeling my kitty jump at the vibrations of his voice, I happily obliged and put my leg up on the edge of the shower. Jacier wasted no time crouching down to eat my pussy. He blew on my clit before sucking it into his mouth. My body began to shudder as he inserted his finger in me. He started to move his finger as if he was beckoning me to him, and the shit drove me crazy.

"Jacierrr," I moaned out.

"Mhm, give it to me," he said, never letting my clit leave his mouth.

I placed my hand on his head to push him back a little because I wasn't ready to cum yet, but Jacier wasn't having it. He slapped my hand away as he continued to feast on my pussy.

"Ohhh, fuckkkkk!" I cried out as my leg started shaking while I released right there in his mouth.

Making sure he didn't miss a beat, Jacier made sure he licked up every drop of my juices. When he was done, he came up for air with a wet mouth. Being the nasty bitch that I was, I stuck my tongue all in his mouth, tasting every trace of my juices.

"Freaky ass girl." He smirked. "Fucking around witchu, we gon' be late." He shook his head.

I just giggled as I grabbed his body wash and his rag. I commenced to washing his body, making sure I hit every nook and cranny before washing myself up. We quickly dried off before moisturizing ourselves and getting dressed.

* * *

"So as I stated before, there's lots of options. What do you think?" the doctor asked.

When Jacier informed me that we had an appointment, I never would've suspected that it would've been with a fertility doctor. Ever since we pulled up, I had been crying sporadically. They definitely were tears of joy and not of sadness.

I had told Jacier about my fertility issues due to the botched abortion, months ago, and he told me that he would do whatever it took to help me have a baby if that's what I really wanted. He had never lied to me before, so I didn't know why I thought this would be any different.

"Yes, I want to do the treatments," I told him.

"Perfect!" the doctor said with excitement.

He handed me a packet full of paperwork to fill out, telling me that if I had any questions, to not hesitate to ask. My mind was in a whirlwind as I read through all the papers in front of me.

"You okay?" Jacier asked, snapping me out of my thoughts.

"Yeah. It's just a lot, that's all," I told him.

"You know you don't—"

"I want to. I want *this*," I let him know.

He nodded his head. "Okay," he said.

CHARMANIE SAQUEA

Moments later, I was walking out of the fertility clinic with a big ass smile on my face. To know that I was going to be able to get treatments to be able to become a mother was a wonderful feeling.

"What you thinking?" Jacier asked as he pulled out of the parking lot.

"I don't know how I'll ever be able to repay you," I told him.

"Repay me? Whatchu talking about?" he asked.

"You came into my life and did everything that you said you were going to do. I told you about my fertility issues, and you never judged me. Instead, you came up with a solution to help me with my problem. Even though we had a small break, you still kept your word," I explained.

"That's just the real nigga in me, Princess Lay. Just because we had a little interception in our relationship don't mean I was going to switch up on you. If I don't have nothing else in this world, I have my word. Word is bond. If I tell you I'm gon' do something, please believe I'm gon' do it," he said.

"I know, I know. I just wasn't expecting you to do this."

"Everybody deserves to be happy, Princess Lay. I could tell by how you interact with everyone else's kids that you really yearn for your own, and I wanted to be able to make that happen for you," he said.

"You're so perfect," I told him as I wiped the tears from my eyes.

"I'm far from perfect, shawty," he corrected me.

"That may be true, but you're perfect for me," I told him as I leaned over to kiss him.

I honestly didn't think things between Jacier and I could get any better, but he always seemed to find a way to amaze me more and more each day. The little time we spent apart from each other didn't do anything but make us closer. My brother was right; the whole time I knew Jacier was who I wanted to be with, but I didn't know how Santos would take it. I was happy that we were able to part ways peacefully because both men really meant a lot to me in their own ways.

22

Cherokee

*A*fter applying my last coast of lipstick, I did a once over in the mirror to make sure I was well put together. I was representing my husband tonight, and I didn't need not one strand of hair out of place. Satisfied with how I looked, I grabbed my clutch so we could go.

"Damn," Dillinger and I said at the same time.

My man, excuse me, my *husband* was the epitome of fine. He stood before me dressed in all black. He had on an Armani shirt to go with his Armani slacks, and black suede Stacy Adams loafers adorned his feet. The only jewelry he wore was a gold Cuban link chain that sat against his chest since the first button of his shirt was left undone.

"You got me about to say fuck this party. I got other things I would rather do tonight. Like you for instance," he said as he walked over to me.

"Dilly, no," I whined as I backed away from him. "I spent too much time doing my hair and makeup for tonight. Not to mention all the time I put into planning this retirement party for you." I rolled my eyes.

Yes, Dillinger was still having his retirement party because, for all the streets knew, he was in fact getting out of the game. Nobody but the people near and dear to us knew the truth. Rumors of Dillinger's retirement had been circulating around in the street, so he finally decided to confirm and put the rumors to rest. Everyone was in shock, and a lot of people were indifferent about his decision.

Dillinger meant a lot more to the streets than just another drug dealer, and I was seeing that now. He had taken care of a lot of people, so that left a lot of folks wondering how they were going to take care of themselves and their families. Dillinger did his best to assure everyone that they were going to continue to be taken care of because he left everything to Santos.

"I know, but you look too damn good for me to keep my hands of off." He licked his lips. "Give me a kiss," he said.

"Dillinger, do not play with me right now," I told him.

"Damn, I can't get a kiss from my own wife?" he asked, perplexed.

Sighing in defeat, I leaned in and pecked his lips quickly so he wouldn't mess up my lipstick.

"I promise I'll make the wait worth it when we get home tonight," I told him.

"Yeah, you better." He groaned as we walked out of the room.

"Hermoso, you guys look great together," our nanny for tonight said.

I was very apprehensive about having someone I didn't know watching my kids, but Diego vouched for her and assured me the kids were in great hands. I took his word for it because I knew he wouldn't allow a hair on these kids' heads to be out of place. He even went as far as to get a babysitter for Reign and Nyami for tonight's occasion.

When it was all said and done, I was hoping that Dillinger would be able to work on a relationship outside of business with Diego. He was a little hesitant, but I couldn't blame him. Things like this took time, but I would love for Diego to be a part of his grandchildren's lives since he never got to be in Dillinger's. That was a bridge I would worry about crossing later though.

"Thank you, Lolita. Don't forget, Mateo is not to be up on that game all night. If he gives you any problems, I do mean any, please do not be afraid to call me. Also, Destiny shouldn't wake up anymore tonight, but just in case she does, I left you instructions on how many ounces her bottle should be and how to use the bottle warmer." I explained.

"Si, Señora Rivera, I understand," Lolita assured me.

"Girl, bring yo' ass on. These kids gon be okay." Dillinger fussed.

I rolled my eyes at him as I kissed Destiny, who was sleeping peacefully in her bassinet. I let Dillinger lead me out of the house to the truck that was waiting to escort us to the club. Akil was kind enough to let us host this party at his club tonight.

"Well, how you feeling?" I asked him.

"Shit, like a million fucking bucks," he replied.

"You are so irritating." I laughed. "I was talking about with your decision to take over the throne."

"Oh shit. Still like a million bucks because after tonight, I'm going to be a fucking millionaire." He smiled.

"Will it really be worth it though?" I asked.

"Anything is worth making sure you and my kids are set for life. I don't even give a fuck about me. As long as I know that three of y'all are straight in the event something should happen to me, that's all I care about," he said.

"Stop talking like that," I told him.

"That's real shit though, bae,"

I just looked up at him with nothing but love in my eyes. When I came back to Miami, I never thought that I would be here with him right now. To be honest, I never saw myself coming back to Miami, but due to me running away from Keymar, here I am.

"What yo' pretty ass thinking about?" Dillinger asked.

"About how much I love you," I told him.

"I love you more, Cherry," he said.

And I believed him.

"We're here," the driver said as the truck came to a halt.

Dillinger got out of the truck before coming over to my side to open the door for me. When I tried to get out of the truck, he stood in front of me.

"Thank you," he simply said.

"You don't have to thank me. I told you I was going to throw you a—"

"Not just for this." He cut me off. "For loving me unconditionally, even when I didn't deserve it. I owe you the world," he said.

I smiled as I fixed the collar of his shirt. "And I know you're going to give it to me. Enough of the soft shit. Let's go have fun and celebrate. You deserve it," I told him.

Grabbing my hand, he helped me out of the truck as we made our way into the club. We couldn't even get a foot in it before Dillinger was being swamped. Everyone in attendance wanted to greet Dillinger, shake his hand, give him some dap, or show him love.

"I just got word that the man of the night just stepped in the building with his missus. Y'all show some love for Mr. and Mrs. Dillinger Rivera!" the DJ announced.

The club roared with cheers and excitement, as Dillinger and I made our way up to the VIP section of the club. Once we made it, I stood over the railing, looking down at everyone who was in attendance to show the man of the night some love. *My* man.

This was it. After tonight, our lives were going to change for the better.

After Dillinger had enough turning it up, he decided that he wanted to get on the mic and say something before the night was over. I sipped my champagne as I watched him walk over to the stage.

"I just wanna thank y'all for coming out to show a nigga some love. This shit really means a lot to me. I want to thank my wife even more for making this night as special as it was. I love you, Cherry," he beamed.

"I love you too, baby!" I yelled, causing everyone to roar with laughter and cheer.

I was tipsy as fuck and couldn't wait to get my husband home so we could get nasty.

"Alright, that's all I wanted to say. Make sure y'all stop by the bar and get you a drink. I'm feeling generous tonight, so it's all on me," he said.

My body tensed up when I saw a red dot on his chest. Before I could even yell out to him, the club erupted in pandemonium.

Pow! Pow! Pow!

"Dillingerrrrrrr!" I screamed at the top of my lungs.

"Cherokee, get down!" Akil yelled as I tried to run for Dillinger.

"Noooo! Get off of me! I have to get to my husband!" I yelled as I fought to get away from the guard who had me.

Dillinger's body was just lying there on the stage while everyone trampled over each other to get out of the club. Not listening to a damn word I was saying, the guard carried me out of the club through the back. I was hitting him all in his back as I tried to get him to put me down.

When we finally made it outside, Santos came over to me.

"I got her," he told the guard.

"Cherokee, Cherokee! Look at me!" Santos yelled as he shook me.

"We need to get you out of here, it's not safe," he said.

"No, I'm not leaving him." I shook my head.

"C'mon on now, Cherokee. Did you forget who the fuck you talking to. You know damn well I'm not going to leave him here. I got him," Santos told me just as Layla and Jacier ran over to where we were.

"Come here," she said as she pulled me into her arms.

"They didn't have to do him like that, Lay. They didn't have to do that." I cried.

"Can y'all make sure she gets home?" Santos asked them.

"Yeah, yeah, I got her," Jacier told him.

"I told you I'm not leaving my husband," I spat.

"Cherokee, there's nothing that you can do for him right now, shawty. I know you don't wanna leave, but you have to," Jacier said.

Finally giving in, I let him pull me away to his truck. The whole ride home, I cried on Layla's shoulder. I couldn't believe that a night that started off so impeccable turned into a disastrous one in the blink of an eye. Who the fuck would want to kill Dillinger right before he retired from the streets? He was no longer going to be a threat, so why come after him?

EPILOGUE

CHEROKEE

I wiped the tears that fell from my eyes as I placed the flowers on the headstone. I was trying so hard not to break down, but it was easier said than done. I didn't think this shit was ever going to be easy.

"We miss you like crazy. You should see Destiny now. Her little grown but is almost nine months and trying to walk. I can't believe how fast they're growing. Mateo is doing wonderful in school. In fact, he's on the honor roll. Every day, I make sure they know you and know who you are," I said as I wiped the tears that wouldn't stop falling. "I love you," I whispered.

Getting up from the grave, I slowly walked over to the awaiting car. Sighing, I got in the car as it pulled off. I laid my head back on the seat, just looking out the window as I thought about how much my life had changed in the past few months.

I was living on a high with the man that I loved; nothing could knock me down, or so I thought. That night at the club, I knew my life was going to change forever, but I never would've expected it to change like that. That night Dillinger died at the hospital, my world came crashing down around me.

I fought so hard every day not to fall into a deep depression, but I had to continuously remind myself that I had two children I had to live for. They really were the only thing that kept me going.

"We're here, Mrs. Rivera," the driver announced.

I was so caught up in my thoughts that I hadn't realized we had reached Diego's already. The night Dillinger got shot, we got close and formed a very good bond. He was an excellent grandfather to Destiny and Mateo, as well as his bonus grandkids that he took in. Reign and Nyami loved Diego, and he loved them just like they were his own flesh and blood.

"Girl, it's about time. I thought I was going to have to come get you." Layla fussed once I walked into the kitchen.

Today was Diego's birthday, so we were all at his compound to celebrate.

"Calm down, big mama. You know I would never miss a celebration as such," I said as I rubbed her stomach.

My best friend was six months pregnant with her miracle baby. The IVF treatments she had been going through were a success, and she wasted no time getting knocked up. In just three short months, her and Jacier will be welcoming a baby girl.

"WHERE'S POPPA?" I asked.

"Outside with those hyper ass kids, girl. You knew that." She laughed as we made our way outside to join everyone else.

"C'mon, y'all, so we can sing happy birthday to Poppa!" I yelled out to them.

"Girl, how the hell you showing up late barking orders?" Santos asked.

I stuck my tongue out as I gave him the middle finger. He was here with his new girlfriend Neveah. She was cool and kept his ass in check. That was exactly what his ass needed.

"How did it go?" I heard from behind me as strong arms wrapped around me.

I sighed as I melted into his chest.

"It went exactly how I expected. I cried like a damn baby," I told him as I turned around to face him.

I smiled brightly at Dillinger. That night he died at the hospital, they were able to revive him, but he coded two more times before they were able to get him stable. Not only that, but one of the bullets had hit his spine, paralyzing him. Dillinger was determined to be able to walk again and had been putting in major hours in physical therapy. So much so, that he was able to get around now with a cane.

Unfortunately, Dillinger's attempted assassins are still unknown and on the loose. We had been staying here at the compound with Diego until he felt like his son was well enough on his feet to handle what needed to be handled. Since the shooting, Diego and Dillinger were able to start working on their relationship. They understood they could never get those years back that they spent apart, but they were making up for it. Diego never left his son's side while Dillinger was recovering, and I commend him for that.

"That's okay. I know you miss her, hell, I miss her too," he said as he kissed my lips.

Not only was today Diego's birthday, but it was also the anniversary of my mama's passing. That was the first time I had been to her gravesite since her funeral, and it was still hard for me to believe that she was gone.

"Are y'all gon' keep locking lips or are we gonna eat some cake and ice cream?" Layla asked, interrupting our moment. "Let me know something," she said.

"Shut up, fat ass," Dillinger and I said at the same time, causing everyone to laugh.

"Aye, y'all better chill on my shawty. I actually think she looks good as a fat girl," Jacier said.

"Jacier, really?" Layla squealed.

"Chill. I'm just playing."

"Oh Lord, here her cry baby ass go." Santos rolled his eyes.

I couldn't help but to laugh. This was the shit I lived for. All of my family in one place, happy and enjoying each other. It took a lot for us to get here, but we made it nonetheless. If I had to go back and do it all over again, I swear I wouldn't change a thing.

The End

ABOUT THE AUTHOR

Born and raised in Kalamazoo, MI, Charmanie Saquea's love for writing began in high school after taking up a creative writing class. She pinned her first novel Official Girl at just 18 years old and since then has gone on to pin 30+ more novels. In February 2018, she welcomed her first child. After a taking a hiatus to be a mother, she is back and ready to bring more heat to her readers.

Stay Connected:
Readers Group: Charmanie's Queendom

Royalty Publishing House is now accepting manuscripts from aspiring or experienced urban romance authors!

WHAT MAY PLACE YOU ABOVE THE REST:

Heroes who are the ultimate book bae: strong-willed, maybe a little rough around the edges but willing to risk it all for the woman he loves.

Heroines who are the ultimate match: the girl next door type, not perfect - has her faults but is still a decent person. One who is willing to risk it all for the man she loves.

The rest is up to you! Just be creative, think out of the box, keep it sexy and intriguing!

If you'd like to join the Royal family, send us the first 15K words (60 pages) of your completed manuscript to submissions@royaltypublish-inghouse.com

LIKE OUR PAGE!

Be sure to <u>LIKE</u> our Royalty Publishing House page on Facebook!

CPSIA information can be obtained
at www.ICGtesting.com
Printed in the USA
LVHW111740190419
614855LV00001B/119/P

9 781092 592222